DR

West Stenning Manor is the house of a thousand story books, of concealed passages, hidden treasures and highwaymen visiting beautiful women by moonlight. So thinks Hannah. But the manor is now a course centre, and Hannah is allowed to go there only because she helps with the chores – and keeps Dina away.

For Dina the house offers the tantalizing prospect of glimpsing the celebrated people who come to teach in it. And her dreams seem to come true the day a famous television actor arrives to tutor a weekend course, with his rude and demanding daughter Julia unexpectedly in tow. There's no room at the manor for Julia, so it is arranged that she will stay with Dina's family.

But Julia is not to be so easily deprived of her father's attention. Before long Dina begins to realize that famous people are no better than ordinary ones, and Hannah fears that she'll never be allowed back to the manor.

Meanwhile Tom, Hannah's brother, has his own vision of West Stenning Manor. Although seemingly in a world of his own, he becomes increasingly fascinated by the complex drama being enacted around West Stenning.

Dream House is one of the most entertaining and satisfying stories yet from the author of the Carnegie Medal winners *Thunder and Lightnings* and *Handles*.

Jan Mark was born in Hertfordshire and grew up in Kent. After study at Canterbury College of Art she taught art in Gravesend. She now lives in Oxford.

Other books by Jan Mark

AT THE SIGN OF THE DOG AND ROCKET
DEAD LETTER BOX
THE ENNEAD
FEET AND OTHER STORIES
FRANKIE'S HAT
HAIRS IN THE PALM OF THE HAND
HANDLES
NOTHING TO BE AFRAID OF
THUNDER AND LIGHTNINGS
TROUBLE HALF-WAY
UNDER THE AUTUMN GARDEN

Jan Mark

Dream House

Illustrated by Jon Riley

Puffin Books

PUFFIN BOOKS

Published by the Penguin Group
27 Wrights Lane, London w8 5TZ, England
Viking Penguin Inc., 40 West 23rd Street, New York, New York 10010, USA
Penguin Books Australia Ltd, Ringwood, Victoria, Australia
Penguin Books Canada Ltd, 2801 John Street, Markham, Ontario, Canada L3R 1B4
Penguin Books (NZ) Ltd, 182–190 Wairau Road, Auckland 10, New Zealand

Penguin Books Ltd, Registered Offices: Harmondsworth, Middlesex, England

First published by Viking Kestrel 1987
Published in Puffin Books 1989
1 3 5 7 9 10 8 6 4 2

Made and printed in Great Britain by
Richard Clay Ltd, Bungay, Suffolk

For
Mary Mitchell

Chapter One

Major Nevard rose from his desk and stretched. Long hours of bending over military documents had left him stiff. You could tell by his weary sigh as he stood up that he was sick of sitting in an office and longed to be out on the battlefield, leading his men (who would follow him anywhere) into combat against the enemy.

Hannah was not sure whom the enemy might turn out to be, nor where the battle would be fought. She was even confused about which war was going on because she had missed the first episode, but it was quite certain that Major Nevard was an officer and a gentleman; definitely British because when he went out of doors he was in London – sometimes you saw Nelson's Column in the distance – definitely a gentleman because of the way he talked. Forty minutes of listening to the major had convinced Hannah that she herself knew no gentlemen. She had never met anyone who talked quite like Major Nevard.

The major switched off his desk light, walked over to the window where he drew aside heavy curtains, and looked out into the night, over the silent city. The windows were criss-crossed with sticky tape (it must be the Second World War, Hannah decided; they had done the Blackout at school) and the major's view was cut up into little triangles. Suddenly, towards the dark horizon, a pillar of light sprang up, eerily swinging across the cloudy sky. Although it was not shining on the major his face showed pale against the window, grim and determined. He frowned, head bowed, and as he drew the curtains Hannah heard the anguished crooning of an air raid siren. The screen went blank.

Only seconds later – or perhaps it was next evening, it was hard to tell – Major Nevard sat with his wife on the settee by the gas fire in their flat. Hannah knew that it must be a flat; no ordinary living-room would have so many doors. Mrs Nevard looked sadly at her beautiful red nails and said she would get a job in an aircraft factory. Major Nevard frowned, as he so often did when he was about to speak, and said that he hated pulling strings but Mrs Nevard's father, the general, must try and get him out of that office. He wasn't going to spend the war driving a typewriter.

'Darling, didn't you do enough last time?' cried Mrs Nevard, for the major walked with a limp as the result of an old wound. Mrs Nevard often referred to the old wound, almost affectionately, as if it were a tiresome family pet.

'Is the Old Wound playing up?' she would inquire, and sometimes he slapped it, as you might slap an excitable dog, but tonight he only winced and Mrs Nevard looked tenderly concerned. Then he and Mrs Nevard kissed each other a bit, in a moody sort of way, partly, you could see, because it was wartime, and partly because they had been married a long while, and then Mrs Nevard said, 'Thank God the boys are out of it,' sighing deeply. Hannah had already worked out that the boys had been sent to the country out of harm's way, for Mrs Nevard kept ringing up her sister-in-law to ask how they were. It was a pity. Hannah would have liked to see some children occasionally. At last the Nevards stopped kissing and got up to go to bed. The major did not mention the Old Wound – he was very brave about it – but he groaned and thumped his thigh and then said that perhaps Mrs Nevard could ask the general to dinner.

There was a bit of dickering about ration books after which Mrs Nevard said, 'I'll phone Mummy tomorrow.' She looked older than Hannah's own mother and Hannah had stopped calling *her* 'Mummy' years ago. Privately Hannah thought that the major had made a grave error of judgement over Mrs Nevard, but he was devoted to her. He took her hand and kissed the glossy nails.

'Soon it will be engine oil, not Scarlet Sin,' he said, strangely.

'It will seem awfully queer,' said Mrs Nevard. 'I hope I don't regret it.'

'You'd regret it if you didn't,' said the major. 'And it's your decision.' He mentioned decisions rather often. The serial was called *Decisions*. Darkness fell and the credits rolled, while the sirens moaned.

'Megatripe,' Karen remarked, from where she was sprawled on a bean bag. Hannah switched over for the News, before Dad could come in and tell her to, and wondered how her sister was able to tell what kind of tripe it was. Her ears were muffled by the headphones of her personal stereo and every time Hannah had looked at her, her eyes had been shut. 'Dunno what you want to watch it for.'

Dad came in for the News and Hannah went to help Mum make coffee. She was not in the least interested in Major Nevard, nor his war, nor his wife, nor his Old Wound, any more than Karen was, but in a week or so she would be meeting the actor who played him and she wanted to find out what he was like. Now she knew; decisive.

Testing. Testing. Five, four, three, two, one. Zero. The quick brown fox jumps over the lazy dog. This is Dina Swain. This is Geraldine Marie-Elizabeth Swain, OBE, Ten, Pilgrims' Close, East Stenning, Kent.

I bet I am the first person who ever thought of keeping a diary on tape. I can't be bothered writing, it takes too long and by the time I've worked out how to spell a word I've forgotten what I wanted to say. I was going to start keeping a diary when they opened up West Stenning Manor and I wanted to make a list of all the famous people I met, well, I've got a list but I meant to tell what they were all like and that's what I'm no good at. It's like at school, I always get Good for oral, but if I write things down it's all Tipp-Ex. Talking's easy and when I want to remember what's happened I can just play back the tapes. I shall call them the Swain Tapes. I could bury them in a time capsule with a photograph and in a hundred years people would dig them up and know what I was like. And they'd know who was famous in 1987.

Oh.

Monday, August 3rd, 1987. This way I can do the diary after I've gone to bed and Mum's made me put out the light. What I'd really like is one of those Walkmans like Karen Fisk's got, but I don't know if you can talk into them. Auntie Moira gave me this little radio cassette recorder for my birthday, and some blank tapes. I expect she thought I would record pop songs on them, but this is better. I wish I knew who was going to be at West Stenning next week. All the people who teach there are famous but they aren't famous like you get on telly, they only write books or paint. Sometimes there's musicians but not superstars or anything. I've never heard of any of them but Mrs Fisk says they're famous and she works there so she ought to know.

I got a brilliant top for my birthday, really mega, it's bright pink with big black dots and I got this mega hat in Ashford market with a shiny black bit in front. I'm going to get some mirror shades too, really mega, with what's left over. Becca Stilwell lent me her high heels but I can't cycle in them very easy. I wish we lived somewhere flat.

I feel really stupid talking to myself like this.

Tom Fisk was supposed to be asleep, but he had been looking at his map of the Stour Valley Interchange by torchlight, and his eyes were full of swooping white ribbons of concrete, knotting and twining, over and under, a labyrinth of carriageways.

Next to the map, green and bilious in the light from the street lamp outside, hung his bird-watching chart, the detailed illustrations reduced to dark hazy blobs that tapered at one end, making it impossible to tell a kestrel from a goldcrest. Since the time two years ago when he had spent a day in bed identifying visitors to the snow-bound bird-table in next-door's garden, everyone assumed that he was interested in ornithology. He was always being given bird books, bird calendars, bird charts; people sent him postcards with birds on. Even his binoculars were supposed to be for watching birds, so Gran had said when she gave them to him. As he did most of his bird-watching on the downs, away from the house, no one ever saw him erect the tripod made from purloined fencing stakes, lash the binoculars to the top of it, and transform himself into a surveyor with a theodolite.

Last Christmas Gran had followed up the binoculars with *The Wonder Book of British Birds*. At the front of this was a useful diagram of what a bird looked like inside, in case you ever needed to know. Tom had never been all that curious about birds in the first place, let alone about their interiors, but the layout reminded him of a picture he had once seen at school; an aerial photograph of the Gravelly Hill Interchange, near Birmingham: Spaghetti Junction.

It was out of this small coincidence that he had developed his audacious plan to link the M2 with the A20, a network of roads and viaducts striding across the heart of Kent, fed by sliproads. He was sure that eventually Kent would be just like this, especially if they ever got round to digging the Channel Tunnel, and he saw no reason why he should not be part of the grand design, if he got in on the ground floor, in which case he would make sure that one of the sliproads led up from the village. They could be in France in a couple of hours.

He fell asleep wondering if bicycles would be allowed through the Channel Tunnel, and pedalled doggedly into the darkness.

Dear Mummy, don't try to find me. I don't suppose you will because nobody cares about me anyway. I shall come back when I'm ready and I shall be quite safe, not that you'd care if I wasn't. Love, Julia. PS. You needn't call the police

No, that wouldn't do. Mummy would call the police anyway, immediately. She might even call them before she found the note. The first bit was good, though.

Dear Mummy, don't try to find me. I don't suppose you will because nobody cares about me anyway. I was supposed to stay with Daddy this weekend and that's what I'm going to do. I know you don't really care where I am

No . . .

Dear Mummy, I know you don't care where I am so don't try to find me. I'm quite safe and I'll be back on Monday

No; that would mean the police again. And if Daddy knew what she was planning he would make sure that it never happened. Somehow she had to get to Oxford, and Daddy, before Mummy noticed that she was missing, and then hide in the car and only come out when it was too late for him to send her back; unless he was going by train. He would have to come through London.

She leaned from the window, looking out over the city, roaring and purposeful even at ten o'clock at night. She had switched off the bedside lamp ages ago, in case Mummy saw light under the door and came in to see what she was up to, but with her writing pad balanced on the window sill there was light enough to see by coming from outdoors; from the street lamps, the windows of the houses opposite, the sullen orange glow that never left the sky all night. Only the brightest stars could pierce it.

Daddy hadn't been to West Stenning before but he said that in the country you could see stars rising over the horizon. She imagined the house, great and grey, couched among formal gardens with clipped box hedges and blazing flower borders like they had at Blickling Hall, and all around it rolling parkland where shy fallow deer flickered like shadows under the ancient trees. She had heard him say that he looked forward to getting away from things for a bit at West Stenning. Ha! Little did he know.

Dear Mummy, I have gone to West Stenning with Daddy. I'll see you on Monday. Love, Julia. PS. I know you don't really care where I am. PPS. Don't try to bring me back, I

Well, something like that. She had a week to work on it.

Chapter Two

Hannah, looking out of the window, saw a man with four legs running across the brow of the hill. If Tom had been in the house she would have called him up for a loan of his bird-watching binoculars, but Tom, and the binoculars, were over at the quarry. Hannah stood on the edge of the bath and leaned further out of the window, ready to catch another glimpse of the runner when he should appear, as he surely must, at the cattle grid where, if he was what he seemed, he was going to be in trouble. The cattle grid was designed to stop people like him, people with hooves; sheep mainly. The sensible part of Hannah's mind told her that there were no centaurs roaming the North Downs, but she could not deny that unsettling silhouette against the blue sky; two strong forelegs, seen from the knees up, pumping athletically, and two jigging at the rear, oddly shrunken. She was glad that she had seen it at ten in the morning and not at sunset, with a long night ahead in which to worry about it.

The centaur jogged unhindered over the grid and it was only George Ballard, out for his morning run, his grey sweater knotted at the waist so that the arms hung down behind, bobbing and jerking at every step; neither centaur nor satyr. George vanished again behind the barn. In a moment he would thump across the courtyard, nip into the outhouse for a shower and then back again, to join Mum in the office, which left Hannah with just enough time to sprint downstairs to the kitchen, switch on the kettle and make coffee. George took his showers, as he took everything else, at the gallop. She had five minutes.

The stairs were wide and shallow, with oak newels at the foot of the banisters, leading down to the stone-flagged hall. The dining-room was also stone-flagged, the grey slabs reaching to the very back of the great fireplace where you could stand staring up the chimney at the sky, seeing isolated stars at night or a diamond-hard planet, framed in the flue. The kitchen floor was quarry-tiled but most of the space was taken up by the long deal table on which the course members prepared their meals before cooking them in an oven the size of Hannah's school kiln. Exposed beams ribbed the ceiling where tall people regularly cracked their foreheads, especially first thing in the morning before they were properly awake.

There were three electric kettles. Hannah, who knew them intimately, switched on the fastest. The three mugs were already primed with instant coffee, one with sugar for George, who needed the energy, and while the kettle boiled she went to stand in the open doorway, looking across the yard to where the cats, in the sunshine, were closing in on a rodent hidden in the long grass. They always worked as a team, Martha flushing out the prey, Bertha jumping on it. If Ogmore, their ginger brother, hove into view, they would leave off the hunt and beat him up because he tripped over twigs and frightened the game. Bertha was the brains of the outfit. All summer she had been sitting in the yard watching the housemartins' nests, the swooping birds, calculating the angle of glide. Ogmore caught worms and laid them on the doormat, alongside his sisters' mice. Once he brought home a small rabbit but Polly said he must have sat on it by mistake.

Hannah leaned against the whitewashed wall of the porch; before her the sunlit yard, the shining grass in the paddock, white sheep grazing on the hillside; behind her the cool low rooms, housemartins under the eaves, starlings in the thatch. West Stenning Manor was the house of a thousand story books, where children on holiday found secret panels, concealed passages, hidden treasure, lost documents; where huge families comprised mainly of identical twins, enjoyed wonderful Christmas parties round blazing logs; where beautiful girls in satin parleyed with highwaymen from thatch-shadowed windows. Every time she ran down the staircase she felt long silk petticoats balloon and swish round her ankles. When she stood in the porch she always pushed up her sleeves like a country wife resting from a long stint at the butter churn. There was only one thing wrong with West Stenning, from Hannah's point of view. She didn't live there.

When she barged backwards into the office, hands full of coffee mugs, George was there before her, wound up in the telephone flex because he could never stand still, even when he was talking. With the receiver at his ear the flex went once round his neck and under his left arm; he had already turned round twice since answering the telephone. Mum was sitting at her typewriter, head bent low out of reach of George's elbows. The office was so small that if Polly turned up Hannah would have to go out again. Much as she liked Polly, Hannah hoped she would not arrive within the next twenty minutes. The course members did not think so, but to the people who actually ran West Stenning Manor, the office was the hub, the heart, the centre of things, and like any hub or heart, very small compared with what surrounded it. Hannah cherished the rare occasions when she could feel herself at the heart of things instead of an interloper, there on sufferance, and in any case it was a useful place for picking up bits of information, the kind of thing that people said when she was listening because they assumed that she would not be interested.

George unwound himself from the telephone cord, knocking his glasses into the 'out' tray. He wanted to look at the chart pinned to the wall above the copier, but George was gravel-blind without his glasses, which now that he was not wearing them he could not see, groping among the coffee mugs where he thought they might have landed. Mum put them into his hand and he poked them back on to his nose where they hung askew, having only one earpiece. Then he struck out again for the chart, the flex round his waist. The telephone would have followed him only Mum, long ago, had rendered it George-proof by gluing it to the desk.

'Are you going up to the village?' Mum asked.

'We've got one vacancy for the television course,' George said, into the receiver. 'A last-minute cancellation.'

'I'll go back with Polly,' Hannah said, flattened against the door.

'Polly hasn't come yet.'

'Yes, but when she does she won't stay long – it's Wednesday; the laundry. I'll put my bike in the van.'

'Give us a blob,' said George. Mum lifted a round red sticker from a sheet in the desk drawer and handed it to him. George intended to put it on the chart along with nineteen others for 13 August, to show that the Writing for Television course was now fully booked, but in transit it applied itself to his thumbnail.

'I didn't get anything for dinner,' Mum said. 'Can you pick up something frozen from Suzie – it'll thaw by tonight.'

George, even if he didn't have four legs, needed four arms. He was trying to pick the red dot off his thumbnail, hold the receiver and take down a name and address on a pad at the same time. His glasses hung from one ear, and steamed up as he breathed on them. In the distance came the sound of a giant, rattling railings; it was Polly, driving the van over the cattle grid. Hannah saw that it was going to be one of those mornings when leaving would be less painful than staying, took her coffee and slipped away.

Polly Ballard came into the kitchen noiselessly, like one of the cats. She was tiny, hardly taller than Hannah although three times older, and while George crashed about like a rogue windmill, Polly ducked and weaved and got things done.

'Where do you suppose she found him?' Dad had once asked, after watching George put up a camp bed.

'She told me,' Mum had said. 'He was trying to get his bike through a kissing-gate.' Life, for George, was one long encounter between a bicycle and a kissing-gate. Polly disentangled him, time and time again.

'Did George get here safely?' Polly asked. It was only a

mile from the gatehouse where the Ballards lived, but Polly had been married to George for six years. When you came close you could see the frown marks and worry lines on her face, just like Mum's, although Mum had three children and Polly only had George.

'He's wrecking the office,' Hannah said. Perhaps because they were about the same height, Hannah was one of the few people who ever saw what Polly was really thinking. 'Someone's just booked in for that last place on the television writing course.'

'Any more for song lyrics?' Polly said.

'Not yet. Still only eleven.' Hannah unplugged the kettle and poured.

'The tutors aren't well enough known, yet. We'll advertise again. Is that for me?'

Hannah handed her the mug.

'The others got theirs?'

'In the office.'

'Has George poured his into the typewriter yet?' Last week he had poured it into the copier, which had not properly recovered.

'Not when I came out. Are you going straight back with the laundry?'

'You want a lift?'

'I thought I could put my bike in the van. Mum forgot to get the dinner.'

'I'd have thought Karen could have got the dinner,' Polly said. Polly believed that Karen lay on her bed all day painting her toe-nails which was not, in Hannah's view, far short of the truth. They never said as much in Mum's hearing, however. Mum knew perfectly well what Karen was like, but Mum believed that it was an adolescent phase and that she would grow out of it. Polly and Hannah suspected that Karen was just limbering up for a lifetime of painted toe-nails.

'Sling it in the back, then,' Polly said, referring to the bicycle. 'I'll be about twenty minutes.'

She went through to the office, carrying her coffee. Hannah collected her bicycle from where it was propped against the mounting block (where the highwayman would have leaped to his horse), opened the rear doors of the Ford Transit and heaved it in between the seats. Then she went back indoors to fetch out the laundry, piled in plastic bags at the foot of the staircase, for although Polly had not asked her to help Mum had made it quite clear, when she first got the job, that any child of hers who put a toe-nail over the threshold of West Stenning Manor must earn the right to stay. At first she had tried to ban them from the place but George, who liked children, possibly because he had none of his own, had said no, let them come, and in any case, it was only Hannah who cared about coming into the house. Tom preferred the woods and the quarry and Karen was interested only in walking her boyfriends along the footpaths on leafy summer evenings.

The laundry loaded, Hannah sat on the step of the van to wait for Polly. Noises drifted through the open window of the office; George's voice loud and enthusiastic, Mum's low and cautious. Polly, going through the morning's mail, said nothing at all. A squadron of swifts skidded round the side of the house; Martha and Bertha had caught their mouse and were chucking it about in a wasteful manner instead of eating it. They put only leftovers on the doormat.

'Don't play with your food,' Hannah said. Into the yard, very slowly, came Tom on his bicycle, looking through the wrong end of the binoculars.

'You trying to break your neck?' Hannah said.

'Funny, isn't it?' said Tom. 'You'd think things would just seem small, but they look like they're miles away. My feet are like they're on the end of stilts.'

'Have you come all the way from the quarry like that?' For all she knew Tom might well have been *climbing* the quarry with the binoculars reversed. Grown men broke their limbs while trying to climb it, from time to time. Tom went up and down on all fours, like a healthy squirrel.

'Just from the cattle grid.' Tom turned the glasses and looked back up the lane towards the brow of the hill, where George had earlier come into view on four legs. 'Bandits at twelve o'clock,' said Tom.

Just breasting the hill was another cyclist. Hannah grabbed the glasses and focused on the slowly pedalling figure.

'Drippy Dina?' Tom said.

Hannah handed back the binoculars and pulled her bicycle out of the Transit.

'Going to head her off?'

'Tell Polly I decided not to wait,' Hannah said.

Tom nodded. He understood.

'And don't say anything to Mum.'

Tom understood that, too.

Dina was wearing jeans and a T-shirt because it was Wednesday and the week's course had not begun. When the courses were on Dina wore bright pink shirts and striking hats, and rode her bicycle dangerously in spike-heeled shoes. She braked when she saw Hannah come round the corner over the cattle grid, standing on her pedals. The lane climbed steeply from there on.

'You going home already?' Dina said, disappointed, as Hannah drew alongside.

'Got to go shopping,' Hannah said. 'Mum forgot to get anything for dinner.'

'Are you coming back afterwards?'

'Don't suppose so,' Hannah said, hoping it was a lie; hoping that Dina would not hang around for so long that it would become the truth. 'Look, there's no one *there*, only Mum and George and Polly. It's Wednesday.'

'Can't you go shopping later?'

'It's early closing, isn't it?' The hardest part of these meetings was actually persuading Dina to turn round. The house seemed to draw her like a lodestone, much as it did Hannah, although for a different reason. 'Come on, I've got enough money. We can have an ice-cream or something. Come *on*, Dina.'

Very slowly Dina dismounted and turned her bicycle, still looking over her shoulder towards the house, as if hoping that something would happen there. Where they were standing the lane had already risen above the level of the chimneys and they were looking down into the yard. Nothing moved there in the quiet sunshine, except for Martha and Bertha, until a figure burst out of the kitchen door, scattering cats, performed some running on the spot and vanished behind the barn.

'George,' Hannah said, firmly. Dina remained stationary. 'Well, *I'm* going,' Hannah said. It was unkind but necessary. Even Dina would not go down to the house without Hannah. Hannah always felt cruel about dragging her away and guilty as well, this time, for as she looked down into the yard she realized that she was seeing what Dina had seen five minutes ago as she cycled over the hill, except that Dina had also seen Hannah sitting on the step of the van, Hannah looking through the binoculars, Hannah taking her bicycle out of the van and riding out of the yard. She must have known why . . . or did she? If she didn't want to know that might well amount to the same thing as not knowing, and she never showed any signs of knowing that Hannah did not like her going to West Stenning.

The hill was too steep here to get up any speed on wheels; even cars that stalled had to roll back over the grid and start again. Hannah walked, and when she looked back Dina was following, still with her head turned to watch the house as it disappeared behind the thorn hedge at the top of the hill. Lord Sherlock's sheep stood in a bland row across the lane staring in the same direction although, being sheep, it was unlikely that they were hoping that anything interesting would happen. Hannah drove them out of the way with rude bleating noises but Dina was deferential and walked round them politely, because they belonged to a lord.

All the land around belonged to the Sherlocks; once, Sherlocks had owned West Stenning Manor and the village too. The present Lord Sherlock lived in London and no one had ever seen him, though Hannah liked to fancy that sometimes he returned in disguise to visit secretly his lands and former possessions, and that the muttering tramp who regularly passed through the village in summer would one day rip off his false whiskers crying, 'Ha! Little did you know! I am Lord Sherlock.' Dina would swoon with excitement.

West Stenning Manor lay in a hollow on the downs. East Stenning, the village, was at the foot of them. The part by the church, along with The Crown and the old pump, appeared on postcards and in guidebooks, for the Pilgrims' Way ran right through the village. Beyond them came the crossroads, with the garage and two shops facing each other aggressively across the main street, and last of all Pilgrims' Close, with its new chalet bungalows and the council estate. This was a crescent of semi-detached houses; Hannah lived at one end, Dina at the other. No one ever put *their* homes on a postcard even though Dina's family had bought theirs and built on a new porch, to prove it.

The two village shops were not really rivals, they just looked as if they must be. The one on the left was both the Post Office and the off-licence, and did very well when the courses were on, but Suzie Mullens, on the other side of the road, kept a good freezer and sold vegetables from her own garden. People who needed something more exciting took the bus into Ashford.

Hannah had propped her bicycle against Suzie's long window sill before she noticed that Dina was still on the far side of the road, peering into the window of the Post Office.

'Over here!' Hannah shouted.

'With you in a minute,' Dina called back, deliberately offhand.

Hannah, growing suspicious, left her bike and crossed the road. The window of the Post Office displayed cards that offered second-hand hamsters and sofa beds, the services of baby-sitters and jobbing gardeners, or promised rewards for lost cats, but sometimes there was a bill pinned up for the amateur dramatic society, or organ recitals in Canterbury Cathedral. Dina was examining a notice that Hannah recognized at once, something that Hannah saw often and took care to keep out of Dina's way. West Stenning Manor published brochures which looked like folded booklets but opened out into a full-sized poster, listing the courses and the people who would tutor them. The brochures had been available since Easter but Mrs Gibson, the Post Mistress, had evidently decided to put one up to catch the eye of summer visitors dropping into the Post Office to buy cards, and stamps to stick on them.

At the top of the poster was a tempting photograph of the house, taken on a sunny spring day although it looked romantic even in January and downright sinister in fog. *West Stenning* it said, *is a sixteenth-century manor house set in rolling Kentish downland, four miles from Ashford and eleven miles from the historic city of Canterbury. Why not join us for a long weekend of writing, music or painting? Courses tutored by professional writers, artists and musicians run from March till October, beginning on Thursdays and ending on Monday morning.*

Dina knew all that. She was looking lower down, at the courses for August, at the two courses in particular that Hannah had been keeping quiet about; *August 13–17: Writing for Television. August 20–24: Writing for Children.* Especially quiet about Writing for Television.

Dina poked the glass in front of the poster. 'Tutors, Gavin Russell and Martin Carter. *Martin Carter?* He's an actor.'

'Yes, but he writes plays as well,' Hannah said. 'And serials,' she added, unwisely.

'Television serials?'

'Yes.'

'But he's *really* famous,' Dina said, and her eyes glazed over, mad and shiny. 'He's in that *Decisions* thing on Mondays, with the horrible wife. I mean, he's really, really famous.'

She dragged her attention from the television course and looked at the details on children's writing.

'Joan Grigson? We've got her books at *school*. We were reading one of them in class, last term.'

'Which one?' Hannah said.

'Dunno. Can't remember.' Dina was not really interested in what people did so long as they were famous for it, and in spite of her passion for distinguished writers, there were no books in Dina's house. Hannah sometimes thought that if you could become a celebrity by sitting for six weeks on top of Nelson's Column, or by swallowing the biggest number of tadpoles in ten minutes, Dina would be first in the queue for your autograph. Unfortunately, although Dina was an avid hunter of autographs, her lust for fame did not stop there. She wanted to be near the famous, hearing them, watching them, worst of all, touching them. When West Stenning had opened up as a course centre she had been unable to believe her luck; celebrities, eight months of the year and less than two miles away. When boring Hannah Fisk's mum got the job as secretary she had immediately set about becoming Hannah's dearest friend. Hannah, as Hannah knew only too well, was Dina's hot line to fame.

It would not have been so bad, Hannah thought sometimes, if Dina herself had wanted to be famous, but she had no ambitions at all, that way. She just wanted to be in touch with people who were famous, as Hannah was in touch with them, only boring old Hannah didn't know when she was well off. All those celebrities and Hannah behaved as if they were just ordinary people.

Hannah had long ago given up trying to convince Dina that famous people were only famous at a distance; close to they were just like any ordinary person. It was difficult to laugh at Dina, she was too much of a threat, but after she had seen Dina queuing at Suzie's freezer behind the man who helped write Dina's favourite soap opera, without knowing who he was, Hannah had laughed on and off all night. This was what she could never make Dina understand – that it was his name that was famous. If you didn't know his name he was indistinguishable from anyone else.

Chapter Three

Any ideas that Hannah had entertained about going back to West Stenning must be postponed. Dina was in one of her hovering moods when nothing short of violence would shift her. Sarcasm had no effect. She waited outside the shop while Hannah bought chops for dinner, and the promised ice-creams, and then walked home with her.

Hannah couldn't fault her for that. It would have been rude to take the ice-cream and ride away, but when Hannah leaned her bicycle against the garden wall, Dina parked hers alongside instead of carrying on to her own house. She followed Hannah up the path and loitered on the step while Hannah fished the key, on its string, out of the letter box. If Karen was home she would be plugged into her personal stereo, deaf to the doorbell. Hannah, as always on such occasions, could not help recalling that before Mum got the job at West Stenning, Dina, who was a year older, had ignored Hannah and refused to walk to the bus stop with her on school mornings. These days Dina would wait at the gate; no matter how late Hannah left it, Dina was always there. They usually ended up having to run for the bus.

'That course starting tomorrow,' Dina said, 'it's no one special, is it? Teaching, I mean.'

'*Tutoring*,' Hannah corrected her, opening the refrigerator. They had form tutors and year tutors at school, who were just ordinary teachers, but at West Stenning there was definitely a difference. The course members were not made to sit down and do things, answer registers and clean the board, They came to write or paint or play music, or at least to try, and the tutors were there to help. 'No, no one special.'

This was not true. The two young men who were tutoring the course were very successful printmakers, but they were substitutes for two famous illustrators who had been booked to come but had cried off at the last moment. As their names did not appear on the brochure Dina was assuming that they must be a pair of no-good upstarts, which suited Hannah very well. Until next Thursday lunchtime she could spend as much time as she liked at West Stenning, not in the house, but *near* it, without Dina bobbing up from the undergrowth in the hope of seeing a poet wandering lonely as a cloud among the daffodils or, at this time of year, among the scabious. Hannah was tired of telling her that it was only the course members who wandered through the daffodils, seeking inspiration. The poets wandered straight up the hill and down again into The Crown.

'But it'll be *Martin Carter*, next week,' Dina breathed.

'He'll be terribly busy,' Hannah warned her. 'The course is full. He probably won't be able to put his nose out of the door once it starts.' Courses on writing for television were always full; a lot of people seemed to share Dina's reverence for television. Whoever it was who had rung up this morning had been extremely lucky to get accepted at the last moment.

'You'll point him out to me, though,' Dina said.

'You won't need me to point him out,' Hannah said. 'You know what he looks like.'

'Well, it would be from a distance,' Dina said, with surprising realism, 'unless you could smuggle me closer.' Dina had seen too many films about teenagers facing fearful odds to get close to the people they admired. Perhaps, in a way, it was better to be like Karen who pasted posters of her favourite pop stars to the ceiling and woke up every morning to find them pouting down at her.

'Aren't you going on holiday next week?' Hannah said, hopefully.

'Week after,' Dina said, 'and not till the Wednesday. Flights to Venice are on Wednesday. I'll miss Joan Grigson, though. You can get me her autograph, can't you? And you'll get me Martin Carter's, won't you?'

'If I get the chance.' This was the unspoken agreement between Hannah, Mum and Dina. If Hannah would get people's autographs for Dina, Dina would promise to stay away from West Stenning, promising not to cross the cattle grid, which was the frontier. Hannah could cross the frontier whenever she liked so long as Dina did not come too. If Dina hung around making a nuisance of herself Hannah would be banned, banished, cast out of Paradise. Dina could be kept at a distance only by the promise of autographs, so it was Hannah who had to lie in wait for the famous, clutching Dina's autograph book, pretending to be star-struck;

knowing that if Mum found out she would get her marching orders.

The kitchen door opened and Karen shimmied in, accompanied by the tinny percussion that leaked out of the earmuffs on her Walkman, and singing in the loud tuneless voice of people who cannot hear themselves.

'Didn't know you were back,' Karen said, when she saw Hannah and Dina. She was not embarrassed; Karen seldom cared what anyone else thought. Tom said it was because she never did any thinking herself; it hadn't occurred to her that other people did. The words of the song she was singing seemed to be *Oo-yer oo-yer oo-love-yer oooo.* People who wandered about wailing 'oo-love-yer' for no apparent reason were likely to be put away, Tom said, but this had not struck Karen either.

Karen ambled round the kitchen assembling her lunch, taking no notice at all of Dina and Hannah. When the holidays began Mum had made some sort of silly suggestion about Karen making lunch for the others when they were at home and the suggestion had never been repealed, but Hannah and Tom knew better than to expect anything prepared for them. Tom lived off the land, sustaining himself through the day on bits of bread and carrots; Hannah, when she could, sneaked a sandwich from the kitchen at West Stenning, but never once a course had started. Stranded now with Dina, far from the manor, she would have to wait until Karen had taken what she wanted and then make a meal out of anything that was left over. At least Dina did not expect to be fed and would go away eventually.

Karen foraged. She carried a plate with a gnawed-looking lump of corned-beef in the middle of it, a lettuce leaf, a heap of bread and margarine and five pickled onions that rolled dangerously about the plate like those balls in a puzzle that have to be manoeuvred into special holes. There is always one ball that will not fit until all the others have become dislodged again, and there was one pickled onion, sliding about after all the others had come to rest on the lettuce leaf or under the bread. Karen left the kitchen dancing a strange slow jive, elbows up, balancing the plate, swinging her hips, eerily yodelling 'oo-yer oo-yer'. She was like a visitor from another world who mistook human beings for furniture and conversed only with machines.

'I'm going to have my lunch now,' Hannah said, pointedly.

'I'd better go then, hadn't I?' Dina said. She did not move.

'Yes . . . well . . .' Hannah said. She opened the drawer of the sink unit and rattled the cutlery in a purposeful manner.

'And you're not going back up West Stenning?'

'Not today.' She crossed her fingers, out of sight among the teaspoons.

'Not later, I mean.'

'Not at all, I don't suppose.'

It was like trying to eat fish with a hungry cat under the table, having enough to share but knowing that the cat would only be back for more, feeling ashamed at being so mean. Hannah knew that Dina did not believe her and would be hanging about all day, watching her every move. How else could she have known that Hannah was at West Stenning this morning? M.I.5 could make good use of Dina. What a pity she did not want to be a spy, but spies, of course, became famous only after they were caught.

Hannah opened the breadbin and took out the stalest piece of Mother's Pride she could find. She scraped a knife round the inside of the margarine tub that Karen had left empty on the draining board and smeared a yellow film over the crust. She held it out to Dina.

'You want to stay to lunch?' Next to the margarine tub was a split tomato, discarded by Karen. She looked thoughtfully at it.

'No thanks,' Dina said. Her mum did field work in summer, picking soft fruit at the agricultural college, but she always left something for Dina's lunch, proper food, to be warmed up, although Dina usually ate it cold, straight out of the saucepan. 'I'll see you later on, I expect.' Sometimes Dina's mum brought home some of the experimental fruit from the agricultural college and Dina would bribe Hannah with it. But Hannah had no trouble in refusing to be tempted by the huge horrible loganberries that reminded her of birthmarks, or the strawberries. The strawberries were much worse, bulging and bifurcated, like scarlet bloomers with yellow polka dots; not like food at all.

Wednesday, August 5th, I found out something today. I bet Hannah didn't want me to know, but I found out anyway. Next week they've got Martin Carter coming to a do a course at West Stenning. He's an actor but it isn't an acting course, Hannah says he writes plays as well. He's in a thing on telly at the moment but he didn't write it. He's brilliant. He's Major Nevard in this war thing and he was wounded in the last war but he still wants to fight in this one so he gets his wife whose father is a general or something to get him into the fighting, although he's got this leg wound and his wife is going to work in a factory and spoil her nail varnish. She's a real wimp. You can see he doesn't really love his wife any more because he's had her so long but he stays with her because he's promised till death and he went to this friend's wedding and when they were saying till death do us part you could see what he was thinking and you could see his leg hurt. He is a brilliant actor.

Hannah better not try and keep me away next week. I suppose I could hide in the bushes like Tom does, no one tells him to stay away. I know what Hannah will say, she'll say he's just ordinary or he's got false teeth or something. She says everybody's ordinary. There was this really dishy poet there last month, he was ever so young, he looked like a singer with a mega flat-top but Hannah said he nicked all the coat-hangers out of his room. I didn't want to know that.

Anyway, everyone nicks coat-hangers. One of mine Uncle Trevor gave me came from the London Hilton.

Hannah got me his autograph but I can't read it. It looks like a squashed crane-fly.

I suppose nicking coat-hangers is ordinary, if everybody does it.

Bye for now.

Julia had circled next Thursday in her diary and written beside the date, RAD: Running Away Day. If Mummy read her diary, as she was meant to do, Julia left it lying around often enough, she would never notice that among all the other feasts and festivals that Julia had so mysteriously marked: SBFWSSD – Stop Being Friends With Sarah Solomons Day; MMWCIHD – Make Miss Winters Cry In History Day; TAOMADDD – Third Anniversary Of Mummy And Daddy's Divorce Day.

She dreamed often of coming into the bedroom to find Mummy guiltily reading the diary. Mummy would quickly slip it into the dressing-table drawer, turning with a little cry, like that idiotic woman who was Daddy's wife in *Decisions* had done when he came in and saw her looking through his address book in the first episode.

'What are you doing, Mummy?' Julia would say.

'Why, nothing, darling,' Mummy would say, and blush.

'You were reading my diary.'

'No, darling. I was just putting it away.'

'I don't keep it in that drawer,' Julia would say. 'I hide it, but of course, you know where.' Then she would turn aside scornfully and close the door, or perhaps she would give a little cry and rush downstairs, sobbing uncontrollably, and fall half-way. Everything going black . . . ambulances . . . a quiet hospital room with flowers . . . Daddy and Mummy holding hands at the foot of the bed, Mummy weeping softly, Julia delirious, Daddy saying, 'We must have no secrets from each other –' no, that was Major Nevard. Daddy would say, 'Why don't you get those stair rods replaced?' and Mummy would snap, 'And who's going to pay for it?'

Julia returned to the bedroom door. 'Reading my diary *again*?' she would say. It was open at the page where she had written in enormous letters I WISH I WAS DEAD!!! Only, if she were dead, she wouldn't be able to watch what happened when they found the pathetically huddled little body. Falling downstairs and a slightly broken ankle would be better.

Chapter Four

Wednesday, August 12th. Hi! I got those mirror shades in Ashford market on Saturday. They look brilliant. I'll wear them tomorrow with my new hat. You can't really see it's me when I've got them on, maybe Hannah won't know who I am; I don't think.

I went round Hannah's just now but Tom said she was out. I bet she wasn't. I could see her bike in the shed, round the back. If I sit on the doorstep I can see when she comes out and catch her up. My bike's faster than hers, it's a Motobecane. I had it for Christmas. Bye.

Between Hannah's house and Dina's lay eight other houses and eight back gardens. The council houses were built in a shallow crescent so that the gardens fanned out, narrow at one end, wide at the other. In winter you could see clear across them but now they were a thicket of bean poles, pea sticks, currant bushes and fruit trees. Dad grew raspberries all the way up the side of the Fisks' chestnut paling fence.

Bending low Hannah ran alongside the canes, plucking off a ripe berry here and there as she went; they were all the lunch she would get. At the end of the raspberries, in the angle of the fence, stood a 'Beauty of Bath' apple tree, good for mistletoe but not for apples, and good for cover. The rubbish heap lay under it, against the back fence. Hannah walked up the rubbish heap, slipping on withered rhubarb leaves like shorn elephants' ears, and jumped, landing in a wasteland of docks and horse-radish.

This part of the hillside was too steep to cultivate; the chalk lay very close to the surface, sometimes breaking through the grass; the bleached bones of buried dinosaurs. Hannah lay flat and began to wriggle forwards. If Dina were in her kitchen she would be too low down to notice anything, but she could very well be in her bedroom, which was at the back of the house and overlooked the hillside where she might not see Hannah, camouflaged in brown and green, but would certainly notice the long grass waving strangely if Hannah disturbed it too vigorously.

The waste ground was almost a hundred metres across and the track which Hannah had worn during the last few months became dangerously exposed at the other end. It would be no good at all in winter.

She looked back, swallowed a last raspberry for strength and good luck, and changed direction, hauling herself hand over hand towards the concrete posts and wire strands of the fence that marked the edge of the wasteland. When she reached that there lay another hazardous ten metres along the lines of the fence, between the grass that grew high but thin and the first furrow of Lord Sherlock's wheat. At the edge of the wheatfield, where it met the corner of Sherlock's Wood, the fence stopped and was replaced by a tall thorn hedge. The hedge was old and Hannah could easily have climbed through it, into the wood, but the undergrowth was sprung with brambly mantraps and treacherously pot-holed under centuries of spongy beech leaves. Moreover, the wood was private, also Lord Sherlock's property. The wheatfield was no less private, and Hannah was a trespasser whichever side of the hedge she was on, but trespassing in the wood seemed in some way much more of a trespass, it was so still and dark; and anyway, it was easier to run out in the open, even if that meant the risk of being seen by Dina. Hannah rose from lying flat, to a crouch, to a stoop, and began to move along the headland towards the crest of the down. Once over that she could stand up and walk. It was a remarkably illicit way of reaching a place where she was entitled to be.

Along the lower edge of the wheatfield ran a perfectly respectable right-of-way, a footpath with signposts at intervals, although they did not point to any place in particular, simply said, unhelpfully, 'public footpath'. Hannah knew exactly where it went. To the left it ran between Sherlock's Wood and Forstall Wood, which was public, and met the Challock Road near the gatehouse where George and Polly lived. To the right it followed the downland ridge between wheat and barley, this year, sometimes oats or potatoes. At the wood's end was a junction where a second path curled casually downhill through sheep pasture. There was a stile here with hawthorn branches arched above it, from where you could look down over West Stenning Manor. As Hannah came along the path she saw a figure perched on the stile, silhouetted against the archway. It was George.

A hedgerow was the safest place for George, where he could do no damage. Hannah called to him while he was still at some distance. If she surprised him close at hand he might jump so violently that he would fall off the stile and damage himself.

'Hallo,' Hannah said.

'Hallo,' said George. They leaned side by side on the stile and stared across the little valley. The path sloped steeply below them, through the pasture, over a little bridge where it crossed Fylde Brook, and entered the land around the manor. George called this the Demesne.

'It'll look all right on telly,' George said.

Hannah often thought the same thing. The thatched manor house was a proper setting for a romantic story, lying in its misty hollow as a stranger rode down to it on horseback through fields of waving corn. Even the sheep could look romantic if you didn't get too close. These visions were always wrecked by thoughts of Dina, springing out of a ditch to get the stranger's autograph. Then she realized that George had said, 'It'll look all right on telly,' not 'It *would* look all right on telly.' She began to pay attention.

'Is it going to be?'

'Very likely,' said George. 'They'll be filming next week. Didn't I tell you? We had a visit from a location manager.'

'What's that?'

'Someone who goes round looking for places to make films in. This one wants to come and use the manor.'

'To make a film in?'

'Not a whole film; just background shots for a particular sequence. It's supposed to be set in Devon but it'd cost too much to take a whole unit that far. They can get here and back to London without too much trouble.'

'But why here?'

'The hills, I suppose,' George said, 'and the thatch.'

'And the sheep. Do they have sheep in Devon?'

'I don't know. I've never been to Devon,' George said. He came from Leicester. 'I dare say they could shift the sheep if they wanted.'

'When are they coming?'

'Monday. Polly doesn't like it, with a course ending. It'd be different if it was a television *acting* course. Still, I don't suppose they'll get in the way,' said George. George was an optimist. Hannah suspected that he might have come up here to avoid Polly. 'It'll please your friend, won't it?'

'My friend?'

'Whatsername? Dina. She'll like the idea, won't she?' George vaulted off the stile and his glasses fell into the ditch. He picked them up and vaulted back on again.

This was just what Hannah was afraid of; Dina getting wind of the news, hanging around, getting in the way, annoying Mum. 'What film is it? Who's acting?' It wouldn't matter to Dina what it was or who was in it. The fact that they were on telly would be enough. Even if they were terribly bad actors, Dina wouldn't mind.

'Don't know,' George said. 'I think someone from one of the courses must have mentioned us. The chap wanted to know if there was a good view from the south so I came up to look. Is this the south?'

'East,' Hannah said.

'But we're south of the manor – I worked it out.'

'But we're looking west, aren't we; look at the shadows. We must be in the east.'

'You mean there isn't a good view from the south?'

'Yes, there is,' Hannah said, 'but this isn't it.'

'I was never any good at Geography,' George said. 'Are you going down?'

'I'm going to help Polly with the beds. I do on Wednesdays.'

'We ought to pay you,' George said. She knew he didn't mean it but it was comforting to know that he thought she was worth paying for and not someone who had to be put up with. He slithered off the stile again and stood aside for Hannah to climb over. While they were talking one of the sheep had wandered over to see what was going on, followed by another and another. Now there was a whole crowd of them standing below the stile and staring up at George and Hannah, patiently, like people at a public meeting, waiting for someone to open the proceedings.

'Women's Institute,' said George.

'Where?'

'These ladies,' he said, waving at the sheep. 'When we first came here Madam President asked Polly to go along to one of the meetings and talk about the courses. I went with her. They all sat round in a huddle and stared at us as if we were going to say something really shattering; you know, the end of the world is timed for Tuesday fortnight. Bring a friend.'

'Where?'

'To the end of the world.' He plunged among the sheep who bounded aside in alarm. Hannah followed him, but it was often hard to follow George's trains of thought. A lot of his conversations were conducted with himself, he asked the questions and supplied the answers, made the jokes and laughed at them. They walked down the pasture; the sheep regrouped and followed respectfully as if they had decided to elect him an honorary sheep. He would make a good sheep, he was so very inattentive, but too energetic.

By the time they had reached the bridge the sheep had thought of a more pressing appointment and wandered away across the pasture. The manor was now out of sight behind the hornbeam thicket through which the path ran, before emerging at the side of the yard at the back of the outhouse. As they came round the side of the outhouse, Hannah could hear Mum's typewriter in the office. Polly stepped from the shower-room door with bucket, cloth and scouring powder, wiping her hair from her eyes with the back of her hand.

'Where've you been?' Polly said, to George, not to Hannah.

'Spying out the land,' George said.

'I'd've thought you knew it by heart already,' Polly said, very snappish. She did not stop to talk but stumped across the yard in her flip-flop sandals, shoulders drooping tiredly. Hannah hoped that George would notice but George, sheep-like, had noticed something more rewarding and was loping across the yard towards the barn which Hannah had helped to clean out yesterday, after the printmakers had used it as a studio. Hannah went after Polly, to the kitchen. The quarry tiles shone wetly where Polly had been mopping them; on the kitchen table, where they were not supposed to be, sat Martha and Bertha, marooned and afraid of getting their paws damp.

'I came to help with the beds,' Hannah said. 'You haven't done them, have you?'

'I haven't had time,' Polly said. She put her bucket on the draining board. 'George was going to do the floors but he got sidetracked in the middle. Someone rang up. No he didn't,' she said, suddenly. 'He got sidetracked after five minutes.' She sat down on the edge of the table and stroked the cats whose moist fingerprints criss-crossed the scrubbed boards.

'Shall I make you a coffee?'

'Please.'

'Was it the television man?'

'Who? Oh, the phone call. Yes it was. I don't want a television crew here, Hannah.'

'Wouldn't it be fun?'

'Fun for them, maybe. You wouldn't believe the fuss. They'll come in a convoy and set up a studio. When they first asked I said Tuesday or Wednesday only, between courses, but George has let us in for Monday. I'm going to be somewhere else when they get here, believe you me,' said Polly. 'It's supposed to be a Christmas scene; can you imagine, filming Christmas in August? I remember the last time I was in Oxford, it was in July but they were doing a winter scene. There was artificial snow all over everything, window ledges and gateposts, and on the street. If anyone comes putting down artificial snow here,' Polly said, 'I shall do something nasty.'

'What sort of thing?' Hannah could not imagine Polly doing anything nasty.

'I'm sure I could think of something,' Polly said. 'I haven't unpacked the laundry, yet. I just left it all in the hall. The floors were so dirty – printing ink.'

Mum came into the kitchen with a pile of letters for Polly to sign. 'What are you doing?' she asked suspiciously when she saw Hannah with the coffee tin. 'She's not being a nuisance, is she?' she said to Polly.

'Not a bit, she's helping,' Polly said.

'Do you want a coffee?' Hannah asked, sounding especially helpful.

'If you're making it. You send her home, Polly, if she gets in the way.'

'She doesn't get in the way,' Polly said, searching for a pen.

Hannah made the coffee wondering if Mum had been a nuisance when she was Hannah's age and if this was why she was so sure that Hannah must be a nuisance. You could be far more of a nuisance, Hannah thought, by not doing anything; look at Karen; look at George. Maybe Mum imagined Polly was just being polite when she said that Hannah was helping, though anyone should have been able to see that Polly needed all the help she could get.

She left them with their coffee and letters at the table, assisted by the cats, and took her own mug upstairs, pausing in the hall to gather up the blue plastic bags of laundry, one containing duvet covers, the other sheets. She could come back for the pillowcases later.

Upstairs the house was just as she had left it that morning, just as it had been last Wednesday between courses, just as it would be next Wednesday, as it would be all year from spring until autumn, every Wednesday; the beds stripped, airing under open windows, the rooms deserted, the bathroom sparkling.

There were five rooms and four beds in each except for those at the back, one of which was tiny with only two beds, and one which was enormous, with six. Hannah went into the six-bed room first, to get it out of the way, because it was her least favourite. She would hate to sleep in there herself, it was like a dormitory, the sort of place where people slept in school stories. Her very favourite she saved until last; the other back room with only two beds. In here the roof sloped, the window was low and narrow with ivy overshadowing it. When Hannah was pretending that she actually lived at West Stenning, this was the bedroom that she chose for herself, and when she had made the bed nearest to the window she lay down on it so that she could recharge her imagination for future reference, gazing up at the steep white-washed ceiling that was divided into strips by the oak rafters. The window was set so low in the wall that she could look out without raising her head from the pillow. Most of the windows in the house were plain glass, but in here they were the kind that people would expect to see in an ancient manor that was mentioned in the Domesday Book, leaded and askew, the diamond panes thick and greenish so that the view from them seemed always to be under water. She was looking towards Forstall Wood beyond the sheep pasture where Tom was sitting, talking to a sheep. Mum never worried about Tom being a nuisance, but then, someone whose idea of a good time was talking to a sheep could not be much of a nuisance anyway. Maybe he was like Doctor Dolittle, and had learned their language.

Chapter Five

The plan was perfect and it did not involve leaving written messages at all; she could do it all by telephone. The whole enterprise was worked out down to the last second on a sheet of paper that really was secret; Julia never let it out of her sight, not for an instant. The diary, lying open on the bedside table, where it had been all day, contained the vital red herring: *Thursday, 13 August. Go to V & A to research holiday project. ASK MUMMY FOR TUBE FARE AND ENTRANCE MONEY!* That was the alibi. If she went by Underground, Mummy would expect her to be away all morning. She would be going to work before Julia got up. Yesterday Julia had rung Daddy in Oxford.

'What time will you be leaving for West Stenning?'

'Not before twelve, love. Why?'

'I'll ring you up and say goodbye.'

'Oh Julia,' he had said, 'I'm only going for five days.'

'You don't *want* me to say goodbye.'

'Of course I do.' She had heard him panicking. She wished that she could cry whenever she wanted to like that woman who was his wife on television.

'Promise not to go till I've phoned.'

'All right, but I *must* leave by twelve-thirty, at the latest.'

That was all she needed to know.

When she woke on Thursday morning the first thing she did was to look at the diary. It lay where she had left it, untouched, she knew, because the hair which she had carefully positioned under it was still coiled into an 'S'. Putting a hair *on* it was a mug's game, everyone knew that dodge, but no one would think of looking underneath. She had heard Mummy creep in at eleven to make sure that she was sleeping peacefully, but evidently she had not stopped to sneak a look at the diary which she would have had to take out on to the landing to read. It was a pity, really, because she had left it open at an especially good page.

Things I hate. 1. Mummy going to work EVEN IN THE HOLIDAYS!!!

She hadn't been able to think of a second thing, offhand.

Today it was very important that Mummy should be at work, and she had already left the house. Julia fished her holdall from under the bed where she had left it, ready packed, and went down to the kitchen. On the table were the breakfast things, a little pile of silver for the tube fare and museum, and a note.

Have a good time at the V & A. Don't forget to lock up. Have lunch out, if you like. Love, Mummy. There was an arrow leading from *Love, Mummy* to a second little pile of pound coins, enough to eat festively at the museum cafeteria. Julia had been banking on Mummy's guilty conscience to help pay for a journey that was going to be much longer and much more expensive than the one from Putney to South Kensington.

It was only a ten-minute walk to Putney Station. Julia timed her exit and arrived at ten-fifty, in time to buy her half single to Ashford. She had tried out the timing the week before when she had gone to consult the rail map of Southern England, which was how she knew that the Ashford trains from Charing Cross stopped at Waterloo East.

In the main station at Waterloo she went into a telephone booth and dialled.

The telephone at home rang three times, then came Mummy's voice explaining that she was out but would the caller wait for the bleep and then leave a message. Julia waited for the bleep and said, just as she had been rehearsing: 'Hallo, Mummy, it's Julia here. I'm at Ashford. I've decided to go and stay with Daddy after all. He did promise me. I know you'd rather be with Michael Atkins *by yourself*. I'll be back on Monday. Bye-bye.'

Mummy would get that message when she came home at four. Julia pressed the blue button by the coin box and dialled again, trembling as she heard the ringing tone in Oxford. Everything now depended on Daddy's having told her the truth when he said that he wouldn't be leaving before twelve.

'Hallo. Martin Carter here.'

'Hallo, Daddy.'

'Oh, Julia . . .' Who did he *think* it was? 'Ringing to say goodbye?'

'No, ringing to say hallo,' Julia retorted. 'Guess where I am.'

'Not at home?' He sounded nervous. Julia prayed that the public address system would not give her away by announcing trains for Southampton and Portsmouth. Apart from that, she'd thought earlier, one railway station sounded very like another.

'I'm at Ashford.'

'*What?*'

'I'm on Ashford station.' She had never seen Ashford station but it must have a phone box on it. 'You *promised* I could stay with you and I'm going to. I'll wait for you in the buffet.'

'Julia . . . for God's sake . . . how could you? *You can't!*'

'I have,' Julia said.

His voice became steely, just like Major Nevard. Who was he trying to fool? 'Then I suggest you get the next train back to London.'

'Haven't got any money,' Julia said. 'I only had enough for a half single and a coffee. See you soon, Daddy. Be quick.'

She slammed down the receiver just as the announcer began to bellow details of the 11.44 to Bournemouth and she knew from the railway map at Putney that you couldn't get to Bournemouth from Ashford.

Julia picked up her holdall and followed the signs out of Waterloo station, over the crossing where taxis snorted like penned bulls, held back by the red light, and continued up the ramp to Waterloo East. She was in plenty of time for the 11.58. It was a nice clean train with a steward who brought coffee and sandwiches along the aisle on a trolley. She bought some of each, making sure that she had enough money to subsidize her long long wait on Ashford station.

Daddy would be down there double quick, but even if he had left as soon as she hung up it would still be a couple of hours before he arrived. And of course he wouldn't have left at once. The first thing he would have done was to ring Mummy, only *his* message would go on the Ansaphone after her own, or anyone else's who had rung in the meantime. When Mummy came in at four and played back the tape and heard Julia's message, she wouldn't be waiting to listen to anyone else. She'd be on the line to Daddy; too late.

All in all, Julia thought, it was almost impossible to take in how clever she had been. The train walloped through Orpington, down into Kent, towards Ashford; towards West Stenning.

New courses began on Thursday afternoons and the course members arrived in time for supper, cooked by George or Polly on the first day. George cooked only if it were a salad.

Dina knew that West Stenning was out of bounds from Thursday onward, but she still accompanied Hannah all the way down to the cattle grid that morning, and when Hannah came out later to empty the office waste-paper bin she was only just wheeling her bicycle over the hill on her way home again. Mum would not be in to work until two-thirty, today. Hannah hoped very much that Dina would have got clear before Mum came cycling along the track to West Stenning and ran into her. She would be perfectly pleasant to Dina, but Hannah would get it in the neck later, when she arrived at the manor.

She was on her way back to the office when she heard the cattle grid rattle. It did not sound like the Ford Transit that drove into the yard, but before she could go out to look the telephone rang. Hannah loved answering the telephone and taking messages for Polly and George or, better still, passing on messages about courses or making reservations (subject to a deposit of twenty-five pounds). Polly was shopping in

Ashford, and although George was officially in charge till she returned, there was no sign of him or the Transit. Hannah lifted the receiver and explained regretfully that next week's Writing for Children course was already fully booked. The lady who had rung to inquire was argumentative, as if she thought she could make Hannah change her mind by nagging and then asking crossly if there wasn't a grown-up she could talk to. Hannah, equally cross, asked her to ring back later and was just hanging up when the office went dark. Something was blocking the window.

The office window was square and high and just now filled with a man's face, looking in. The man was Martin Carter. Hannah recognized him at once because this was how one normally saw him, a head and shoulders framed behind glass – on a television set – but she was surprised because he was not due to arrive until late that afternoon. He made a little porch with his hands to cut out his own reflection, and peered under it. When he saw Hannah he waved one finger, nervously. Hannah understood him to mean that he did not know how to get in and would be very grateful if she came out or else opened the window. She supposed that it was because he was an actor that he could explain so much with just one finger. She had to use both hands to indicate that the window did not open and that she would have to come round to the kitchen door if he wouldn't mind waiting a moment. He nodded and stepped back from the window, and Hannah saw from his expression that he was not alone.

She imagined that he had the other tutor, Gavin Russell, with him, but when she reached the kitchen and opened the door she found that he had worked out where to go and was approaching across the yard accompanied by Martha and a girl of about her own age. He was much smaller than he seemed on television and his hair, which usually looked quite fair, was going grey, but there was no mistaking his voice. He said, 'Good afternoon. You couldn't possibly be Polly Ballard, could you?'

Hannah knew that he meant, 'You can't possibly be Polly Ballard,' but she felt, without knowing how he had done it, that he had paid her a compliment.

'Polly should be here soon,' she said. 'We weren't expecting you till later.' She thought that she should introduce herself. 'I'm Hannah Fisk; my mum's the secretary here. She'll be along soon, too.' She wished that she could return his compliment. 'Aren't you Martin Carter?'

He seemed surprisingly pleased to have been recognized.

'That's right,' he said, 'and this is my daughter, Julia.'

Hannah said 'Hallo.' Julia mouthed something. It was not hallo. There was a 'b' in it. If Julia's father had not been there Hannah would have taken the conversation further, exchanging b for b, but at that moment Martha gave a thin high screech, leaped into the air with drawn claws and wrapped herself around Mr Carter's leg. Then she bit him, just above the knee.

'Martha!' Hannah said, trying to sound shocked, so that he should not think this kind of thing happened regularly. Martha and Bertha always greeted course members and tutors like dear old friends; they were part of the hospitality.

'I must have trodden on her tail,' Martin Carter said, trying to unpick her claws from his trouser leg. 'Poor puss. I'm sorry.'

Hannah knew that he had not trodden on Martha's tail, and she knew who had, and it had not been an accident. She lifted Martha away and held her firmly, looking stern but secretly stroking her because Martha had been the victim of a fell plot.

'Did she get through?'

'Not her teeth. Corduroy's cat-proof, that way, but she's got sharp claws.' He scratched his leg. Hannah knew how itchy cat claws could be.

'Do you want to put TCP on it?'

'No, it's nothing. My own fault.' He tickled Martha contritely between the ears and she beamed forgivingly. Julia looked at her father with contempt, obviously despising someone who apologized for something he had not done.

'If you come into the kitchen,' Hannah said, 'I'll make some coffee.'

'That would be very nice,' he said. 'Do you want some coffee, Julia?'

'I'll stay here,' Julia said. 'You go.' She sounded like someone who was being left to die in the desert while the rest of the expedition forged on to safety. Her father opened his mouth to argue, but Julia turned her back and went to lean on the car. It was not the kind of flash vehicle that an actor might have been expected to drive, but an old Morris Traveller, with beams, like West Stenning Manor.

'Stoop,' Hannah said, leading the way into the kitchen. Martin Carter, following her, might be smaller than she had expected but he was still tall enough to brain himself on a beam. Fortunately he stopped in the doorway and looked round at the kitchen.

'But this is wonderful,' he said.

'It's in the Domesday Book,' Hannah said, switching on the kettle.

'The whole house?'

'The foundations. I mean, there was a manor here when

they did Domesday, but it wasn't this house. Most of this one's sixteenth century – and the rooms at the other end are Victorian. And the thatch was done last year.'

'Do you do guided tours?'

Hannah thought he was serious. 'No, but I could show you round. Well, you'll be staying, won't you? You'll see it anyway.'

'I hope so.' He looked uncomfortable. 'Is there much room?'

'There is for you,' Hannah said. 'There's a flat over the old stable for the tutors.'

'Any spare beds?'

'Not on this course. It's full. Television writing always is,' Hannah said, knowledgeably. She realized what he was getting at. 'For Julia, you mean?'

'If possible.'

'People don't usually bring their children,' she said, severely.

'She wanted to come,' he said, hopelessly. Hannah thought of all the things that she wanted to do when the answer was no, and that was the end of the matter.

'Does Polly know?'

He shook his head. 'I was hoping to see her. It's a bit awkward . . .' His voice trailed off. It was hard to visualize him as decisive Major Nevard as he perched on the edge of the table, folding his fingers together. Hannah had read about people wringing their hands; she had never seen anyone doing it.

'Well, she'll be down in a minute. Milk? Sugar?'

'Just milk, please. Down? Is she upstairs?'

'Oh no,' Hannah said. 'Down from the lodge. Polly and George don't live *here*, they've got the old gatehouse from when this was a – a demesne. Polly says she'd go barmy if she had to live here while the courses were on.'

'I bet she would,' Martin Carter said. He jumped at a sudden clangour outside. 'What was that?'

'The cattle grid. You came over it, just before the barn. That'll be Polly now.' She heard the Ford Transit drive into the yard. Martin Carter slid off the table, wiped his hands nervously and faced the door, but when it opened it was not Polly who stood there, but Mum. She was furious, so furious that she did not notice the presence of a stranger. Hannah did not know why she was furious, but she could make several guesses, and tried to change the course of the conversation before Mum put her foot in it.

'Did you come down in the van?'

'George gave me a lift from the gate. I suppose that's one of your friends out there heaving bricks at the sheep –'

'No!' Hannah said, but not quickly enough.

'Well, you'd better get straight back home, now, and take her with you. It's bad enough that Dina hanging around and getting under people's feet and goodness knows what you get up to down here, I know Polly says you help her but she's only being polite but when you bring people down here and let them do exactly what they like – I asked her what she was doing and she told me –' Mum squared up to Hannah, glaring, '– she told me to mind my own bloody business. If you think you can take advantage of Polly's good nature by bringing people like that here you've got another think coming. You go away now and you stay away. Go on.'

Hannah, appalled, stared at her, wondering how to explain without embarrassing Martin Carter, but one look told her that he was already as embarrassed as he possibly could be. He looked imploringly at Hannah. Hannah wiped her hands on a tea towel and stepped forward.

'MUM! Mum, this is Martin Carter. Mr Carter, this is my mum.'

'I'm sorry,' Martin Carter said, seizing Mum's hand and shaking it before she could get the chance to land one on him, which looked likely. 'I'm afraid that's my daughter out there. She isn't used to the country.'

Now everyone was in the wrong; Mum for insulting a tutor, Hannah for not warning her who he was and Martin Carter for having such an awful daughter. All it needed now was for George to bounce in and say the wrong thing too. In he came.

'Anyone in here own a Morris Traveller?' said George, 'because you parked it in a silly place. I've just run into the back of it.'

The kettle boiled, unnoticed.

Chapter Six

Hannah had learned a lot in half an hour. After George delivered his news she had decided that the most intelligent thing to do would be to disappear, so she sidled out of the kitchen and crept up the back stairs to the bathroom where she set about cleaning the loo, in case anyone should wonder what she were doing there, although the loo had been cleaned quite thoroughly yesterday, by her. From the window she could see down into the yard where Julia Carter was sitting in the front passenger seat of the Morris Traveller, jaw set, staring straight ahead of her. Julia, Hannah thought, was a better actor than her father. She looked as if she had spent all her life rehearsing for today while Martin Carter was behaving like someone who hadn't learned his lines properly. The bathroom was over the front end of the kitchen and all the windows were open.

'Isn't there *somewhere* she could stay?' Martin Carter said, helplessly, and Polly, who had recently arrived, said, 'If only we'd known, we could have arranged something.'

'*I* didn't know till this morning. She was supposed to be going to Wales with her mother this weekend. Then she rang me from Ashford station and demanded to be fetched.'

Hannah tried to imagine what would happen if she went to Mum or Dad and *demanded* something. But life must be different for Julia; Hannah's family presented a united front. One of the things she had learned was that Julia's parents were divorced, and that Julia never saw them together. One of the things she had guessed was that they both felt bad about this and Julia knew it. As she had said to Martin Carter in the kitchen, tutors did not bring their children with them to West Stenning, and he must have known that already, but he was too afraid of Julia to tell her so. There was not a single spare bed in the place and nowhere to put one. The tutors' flat was just big enough for two, and they used it for talking to the course members about their work, in private. The five bedrooms were full. George and Polly had only two little rooms in the gatehouse.

'She could stay with us!' George said, brightly.

'No she couldn't,' Polly said. Hannah had never heard her sound so firm.

'On the sofa?'

'No.'

'Of course I can't ask you to put her up,' Martin Carter said.

Hannah felt very sorry for him, for having Julia in the first place and because he was obviously hoping desperately that someone would say, 'Of course, she can come to us.' For a horrid moment she feared that Mum might say it although, if she did, it would mean that Tom would have to give up his room and sleep with a friend. But there was little chance of that. Tom would not mind a bit but Mum had already decided what she thought of Julia, which was just what she would have thought of anyone who threw things at sheep.

'Hang about,' Mum said, suddenly. 'I've just had an idea.' Hannah felt cold; she actually stopped breathing until she heard Mum's heels clacking on the quarry tiles, out of the kitchen, across the flagstones of the dining-room and the hall, and Mum's voice calling from the foot of the stairs; 'Hannah!'. Then she gasped and it came out in an agonized squeak.

'*Hannah?*'

Hannah went to the top of the stairs. Mum didn't ask her what she was up to, which was what she normally did, she just said, 'Is Deirdre Swain working today?'

Mrs Swain was Dina's mother.

'I don't know,' Hannah said. 'I didn't see the minibus this morning.' The agricultural college sent transport for its fruit pickers.

'Well, have you seen Dina?'

'She came down with me this morning but I made her go back again,' Hannah said, virtuously. 'Didn't you pass her?'

'I didn't see her,' Mum said. This probably meant that Dina had been hiding in the hedge and was still lurking about somewhere.

'I could go and look,' Hannah said.

'No, it's Deirdre I want, not Dina.' Mum turned away and went into the office. 'They've got a spare room.' Hannah, colder than ever, stood rooted at the top of the stairs. Certainly the Swains had a spare room. They had exactly the same number of rooms as the Fisks, but there were five Fisks and only three Swains. A spare room: surely

Mum couldn't be thinking of Julia Carter. Hannah heard the telephone receiver lifted, and slithered silently down a step or two until she could hear what was being said through the closed door.

Mum dialled and then there was only a short pause before she said, 'Hallo? Deirdre?' Mrs Swain was at home.

Hannah could not bear to listen. She tiptoed down the stairs, hands over ears, and went through to the kitchen. The door was open and she could see George and Martin Carter standing together, heads bent, chins on fists, looking at the rear of the Morris Traveller. A few feet away was the yellow Volkswagen Beetle that belonged to George and Polly; the Transit was the property of West Stenning. Polly was sitting at the table.

'Look at them,' Polly said, waving towards the yard. 'Have you noticed how people who aren't going to get anything done tie themselves in knots trying to look purposeful?'

'Is it badly damaged?' Hannah asked.

'No; the Morris has lost a rear light and the doors won't open. We're hardly dented. Do you know,' she said, turning to Hannah, 'I don't like him.'

'I do,' Hannah said.

'Isn't that awful?'

'Why? Because of Julia?'

'Oh no, not because of Julia, although Julia doesn't help. There's a certain sort of man that a certain sort of girl can do anything with. He's one, she's another. Oh no,' said Polly, again, 'Julia's his problem, not mine. Just so long as we get her away before the course members turn up . . . No, I didn't like him from the moment I clapped eyes on him and I've just worked out why. It's not him at all, it's the parts he plays; headmasters, honest cops, True Brits; all those frightfully sensible, straightforward, energetic, efficient types. I can't stand people like that.'

'Is that why you married George?' Hannah asked, thinking that Polly had just given a pretty accurate description of herself.

'Don't cut yourself,' Polly said, tartly.

'But *he's* not like that,' Hannah said. 'I mean, he's a bit of a drip, but he's a nice drip,' she added, for she had not thought him any kind of drip until she had seen Julia in action.

'He's certainly that,' said Polly. She raised her coffee mug. 'Here's success to your ma.'

Hannah remembered the telephone call.

'What's she doing?'

'Finding out if your friend Dina's mum can put up Julia for the next four days. I hope so, because she's certainly not staying here. If she can put up *with* Julia, that is.'

'Can't she go home again?'

'She could be sent – that's no guarantee she'd arrive. What Julia wants, Julia gets,' said Polly, scowling horribly.

They heard the door of the office open and Mum came back. Polly raised her eyebrows. Mum looked at Hannah. Polly shrugged, slightly.

Mum said, 'She'll take her, but I think he ought to pay for her keep. Deirdre doesn't go fruit picking for the exercise and now they've been laid off for a couple of days. That's how I caught her at home.' She turned to Hannah. 'You'd better go and find Dina.'

'I don't know where she is,' Hannah said.

'Then go out to the cattle grid and yell. She'll jump out of the bushes fast enough. She always does.'

Hannah went out, noticing that everyone assumed that she knew what was going on. Did that mean they had all guessed that she had been listening from the bathroom? She left Polly to explain to Martin Carter about their plans for Julia and hoped that Julia had been sitting in the Morris when George ran into the back of it.

'Hannah!'

George and Martin Carter were coming out of the stable.

'Yes?' It was Martin Carter who had called.

'Have you seen Julia?'

'She was in the car just now,' Hannah said.

'She's disappeared,' George said.

'She runs fast,' said Martin Carter, gloomily.

Hannah walked round the corner of the barn and started towards the cattle grid. As it came into sight she stopped. Julia, who was dressed for afternoon tea at the Ritz, was standing on the near side of the grid talking to someone who leaned on a bicycle in the lane on the far side. This person was wearing yellow leggings, a very short leopard-skin print skirt and a pink tunic with enormous black dots on it. There was some kind of hat on her head and fluorescent green discs dangling from her ears. It was Dina, got up in the clothes she wore for celebrity hunting on the grounds that people would stop to look at her even if they didn't like what they saw.

The pattern of the next four days was revealed to Hannah as she approached the grid. Julia might not be a celebrity but she was closely related to one. If she stayed with the Swains, Dina would have no need to haunt West Stenning; just having Julia in the house would keep her happy.

But before Hannah reached the cattle grid the pattern had rearranged itself, as if she had given a kaleidoscope a twist. There was no certainty that Julia would stay away from West Stenning even if she were ordered to, and if that were the case, Dina might come with her. She would not need Hannah any more, Julia would be her passport over the frontier and there would be no way that Hannah could keep her out.

Julia was saying, 'I can go where I like. My father's working here, I don't have to do what *you* say.' She had what Mum called a carrying voice. Although she was speaking to Dina, just across the cattle grid, Hannah, fifty metres away, could hear her quite distinctly.

'Hannah'll tell you,' Dina said. She had just seen Hannah advancing, and meant her to hear.

'Oh, *her*,' Julia said, not bothering to look round.

'I'm just telling her she's trespassing,' Dina said, pleased to have the boot on the other foot, for once.

'Your dad's looking for you,' Hannah said.

'Well, you can tell him where I am, then,' Julia said.

'We've found somewhere for you to stay,' Hannah said, guessing that Julia would not like the 'we'. She was right.

'I'm staying here.' Julia turned at last to face Hannah.

Dina had just put two and two together. 'Your dad? Working here? Who is he?'

Hannah saw where the conversation would lead eventually and that there was no point in trying to divert it. 'He's Martin Carter. This is Julia Carter. She's got nowhere to sleep so Mum's asked your mum if she can stay with you.'

'With her?' Julia's very ordinary face became quite striking with rage. 'I'm not staying with *her*.' She spun round and raced back towards the yard. Dina, not at all offended, watched her disappear round the corner of the barn.

'Martin Carter's her dad?'

It would not matter how awful Julia was, nor how badly she behaved, Dina would love her because she was Martin Carter's daughter.

'Yes, he is, but she doesn't do a thing he tells her. She made him bring her with him and now there's nowhere for her to stay. But you've got that spare room at home . . .'

'Is he staying too?' Dina whispered. All her dreams were coming true at the same moment.

'Of course he's not,' Hannah snapped. 'He's staying here, he's got to. You'd better come down and meet him,' she added. There was no way out of this.

Dina had a wing mirror on her handlebars, but it was not there to warn Dina of motorists coming up behind. She bent down and straightened the hat, which was made of black corduroy with a shiny visor. When she had it at the right angle she took a pair of mirror sunglasses from her pocket and put them on. Now she looked like a mad lady dictator, out for a day at the seaside.

'Dina, he's dead normal. He's not even wearing a tie.'

Dina would not have cared if he had been wearing nothing at all. She propped her bicycle against the hedge and minced across the cattle grid on little high-heeled sandals. When Hannah had last seen her, earlier this morning, she had been wearing jeans and trainers. It was always the same on Thursdays, the lightning change of clothes in case Dina should chance to run into someone famous. At last it had paid off.

When they went down to the yard the scene was very much as Hannah had expected. George was still gazing intently at the rear of the Carters' Morris Traveller, as if he could repair it by looking. Martin Carter was also gazing, at Julia, who was weeping and stamping and screaming, 'You're just trying to get rid of me! Nobody wants me!'

while Mum, pretending that nothing unusual was happening, was giving him directions to Dina's house. Tom used to behave like that, Hannah recalled; when he was about three. Tom himself had appeared from somewhere and was standing a few metres away, watching the proceedings through the wrong end of his binoculars. No doubt that made everything seem pleasantly distant.

'Is that him?' Dina asked, in an idolatrous whisper.

'I'm not going. You can't make me!' Julia shrieked.

'We could run it up to the garage for you,' George said, gently poking the Morris with his toe.

'Just keep going down the main street,' Mum said. 'Straight over the crossroads and you'll come to a cul-de-sac. That's Pilgrims' Close. Number Ten's at the far end – with the fancy porch,' she added, waspishly.

Tom turned the binoculars on Dina and staggered back, clutching his eyes, as though he had been blinded by the colour scheme.

'Darling, everybody's staring at you,' Martin Carter said, cautiously patting Julia on the shoulder and perhaps under the impression that Julia would not want everyone to stare at her.

'I wish I was dead,' Julia sobbed.

Hannah saw Polly standing in the kitchen porch, leaning against the door jamb with her arms folded. She might have been watching a cat fight.

'I wish *you* were dead,' Julia added, in case the message had not gone home.

Hannah was wondering how to break into this charmed circle. She stepped forward.

'This is Geraldine Swain,' she said. 'Julia's going to stay at hers.'

Martin Carter picked Julia off his sleeve, finger by finger, and held out his hand to Dina. For a moment Hannah was afraid that Dina was going to kiss it, but at last she got her strength back and shook hands.

'How do you do,' Dina simpered. 'Sir.' She seemed to give a little at the knees, either overcome with excitement or dropping a curtsy. The leopard-skin skirt was not cut for curtsying. In the background Tom was seen to fall against the Transit, apparently in hysterics although, unlike Julia, he knew how to have hysterics with his mouth shut.

'How do you do,' Martin Carter said, over Julia's head. Julia had decided to collapse and had fallen against him, her face buried in his shirt front. 'It's tremendously kind of you to let Julia stay.'

'It's a pleasure,' Dina said, coyly adjusting her shades. Julia, badly muffled by the shirt front, was understood to say that she wasn't going, they couldn't make her, she would kill herself first. Hannah felt that she had done all she could and left them to it. Polly was still standing in the doorway, arms folded, ankles crossed. Hannah went over to her.

'Can't you sort them out?'

'I can, but I'm not going to,' Polly said. 'It wouldn't last. They'd be at it again in five minutes.'

'They?'

'Carter and daughter. You don't think this is a one-off, do you? She must go on like that every time she wants her own way and doesn't get it. It's not the kind of thing an outsider can sort out, Hannah. The best thing the rest of us can do is stand clear and let them get on with it. I'm just angry with him,' Polly said, 'for letting it happen here. You'll keep her away, won't you?'

'Me?' Hannah said. 'Keep her away? How?'

'How do you keep Dina away?'

'That's different,' Hannah said. 'I know Dina. I bribe her. That won't work with Julia. Dina likes coming here because she wants to meet people. Julia will only want to come because she's not allowed to.'

'You'll all have to find somewhere else to play, then, won't you?' Polly said. The telephone rang in the office and she went indoors to answer it. Hannah stood in the porch and stared after her in dismay, feeling betrayed. She had always thought that she and Polly understood each other, that Polly knew why she came so often to West Stenning; now it turned out that Polly thought she just wanted somewhere interesting to play – as if she ever *played* anywhere. Polly had never noticed how hard she worked to keep Dina away, how hard she worked to earn her place at West Stenning. She had known the house far longer than Polly had, from the time before it opened as a course centre and was little more than a ruin. It had always been hers, but to Polly, she had no rights to it. To Polly, she was just a child whose mother had found her something to do in her spare time. She was no more a person to Polly than was Tom; or Dina; or even dreadful Julia; a child.

Polly came back from the office looking grimly cheerful, which was a more alarming sight than Polly looking grim.

'That was Gavin Russell,' she said. 'George!'

Polly's voice for calling George could stop cheetahs in their tracks. George whipped round and everyone else did, too. Even Julia stopped crying for long enough to find out what was happening. Polly strode across the yard, small and terrifying. 'George, Gavin's just rung from Charing Cross. He'll be on the 16.00; gets into Ashford at just after five. If you drive up to the village now, Martin can follow you and drop Julia and Dina at the Swains'. Then he can leave the car at Twining's, go and pick up Gavin with you and you can all come back here together.'

'That's awfully good of you,' Martin Carter began, although nothing had been particularly good of anyone, but Julia looked up. After that performance her face should have been drowned with tears, swollen and purple, but she was quite dry-eyed and only a little flushed; with exertion.

'I'm not leaving Daddy,' she said, bravely suppressing a sob.

'No, no,' Polly said, pleasantly. 'Daddy's leaving you.'

'I won't go!'

'Won't go to Dina's?'

'No!'

'In that case,' Polly said, tossing the keys of the van to George, 'you can go back to London. George will take you to the station when he meets Gavin. Get your things out of the car.'

'I haven't got any money!'

'We have,' said Mum, Polly and Martin Carter, all at once.

Julia's resistance collapsed entirely. Before she could say anything else Polly was on her way back indoors and Martin Carter, in response to a snap of her fingers, was hurrying to the Morris, to fetch out the suitcase and holdall.

'Famous victory,' Hannah said, as Polly came in.

'Temporary cessation of hostilities,' Polly said. 'Wait till she gets her breath back. Now, let's get on, shall we? Will you do the potatoes or the carrots?' Carrots were a doddle compared to potatoes, but no one who had been offered a choice could choose carrots. Still, Hannah had not forgiven Polly for that remark about finding somewhere else to play.

'Carrots,' she said, because she knew that if she were not there, Polly would have to do both.

Chapter Seven

The carrots and potatoes were washed and scraped, the onions sliced, the stew stewing, by the time George returned. Hannah, watching from the kitchen where she and Polly and Mum were drinking tea, saw Martin Carter and his friend Gavin Russell climb out of the Transit and carry their luggage into the stable. No horses were kept there now; only the Transit, downstairs. Up above were two rooms with a shower cubicle, where the tutors lived during the courses. Hannah was fond of the little flat but it was very new and square inside; she had no sense of living in the past when she was up there and the scent that drifted up the stairs was of oil and diesel, not of hay and horses.

After a few minutes a window in one of the bedrooms opened and Martin Carter looked out. It did not seem to occur to him that anyone might be watching; he propped his elbows on the window sill and covered his face with his hands. Hannah thought about what might be happening up at Dina's house. She imagined Julia Carter lying on the floor kicking and howling, while Dina's mum calmly stepped over her and hoovered round her, and Dina's dad, who worked for British Rail and was on his feet all day, sat in the armchair to watch the News and used Julia as a footrest. He wouldn't be home yet, but Dina had given up kicking and screaming at him years ago. Dina, of course, would be watching, open-mouthed with admiration. It ought to be an interesting evening and she toyed with the idea of dropping by later, to see how things were going.

George came in carrying a case of wine bottles.

'You couldn't send them up some tea, could you?' he asked. 'Poor old Martin hasn't had a thing since he left Oxford.'

'If you'd like to make it,' Polly said. 'Poor old Martin's only got himself to blame.'

'I'll do it,' Hannah said, getting up quickly. Polly and George often argued, quite cheerfully, about whose turn it was to do what, but she had a feeling that any argument today would be for real, and not at all cheerful.

Above the working surface where the kettles stood were shelves of blue and white striped china, enough for two dozen people. The mugs hung on hooks along the bottom shelf. Hannah arranged two on a tray with a milk jug and sugar bowl, a plate of biscuits and two paper napkins. Catering at West Stenning was not usually so dainty, but people always made an effort on the first day of a course. She chose a red enamel pot to make the tea in, out of half a dozen that looked less festive, and warmed it carefully, listening all the while to the conversation that went on behind her.

'What did Deirdre make of her?' Mum said.

'You wouldn't have recognized her by the time we got there,' George said. 'Young Dina softened her up.'

'How?' said Polly, 'with a brickbat?'

'Much more subtle than that,' George said. He was a good mimic. Out of the corner of her eye Hannah saw him become small and fluttery. He clasped his hands under his chin. 'Do you reely live in London? Do you reely go to boarding school? Does your dad ever take you to see him working? You must meet dozens of people.' He sounded just like Dina.

'And how did Madam like that?' Mum asked.

'Madam loved it. She didn't actually answer any questions, she just sort of *expanded*. You could see her thinking, "Hallo, we've got a right one here,"' said George.

'Does she go to boarding school?' Polly said. 'I can't see that kind of performance going down very well. No wonder she lets rip when she gets home.'

'I don't know. She didn't say. I rather got the impression she lives with Mum and goes to Dad at the weekends. This is one of the weekends and she didn't intend to be done out of it.'

'We must make sure it never happens again,' Polly said. 'Joan Grigson's got six . . .'

Hannah could not delay her tea-making any further. She lifted the tray and carried it out of the kitchen, carefully across the yard and extra carefully into the stable where the concrete standing was treacherous with leaked oil. The stairs, only wooden treads, without risers, went up steeply and the door into the flat was flush with the top step, there was no kind of landing; nowhere to put down the tray while she knocked. She had to stand on one leg, propped against the handrail, and kick politely.

It was not Martin Carter who opened the door but the other tutor, Gavin Russell, who was very short and so wide that his elbows touched the door frame on either side. Hannah, who had stepped down a couple of stairs when she heard the door being opened, found herself gazing up at a riotous pullover knitted in rainbow squares like a charity bedspread, and a big black beard. Above the beard was a pair of black-rimmed spectacles balanced on a large lumpy red nose. It was so large that it looked false and Hannah did wonder, for a second, if the whole face was false, nose, beard and spectacles, hooked over his ears. He smiled. His teeth were very white. They too looked false.

'Hallo,' he said, and called over his shoulder, 'Hey, Mart! We're being fed and watered. Come on in,' he said to Hannah.

The smaller of the two rooms had only a bed and a chest of drawers in it. The other had a table and chairs as well. Martin Carter was in there, hurriedly transferring books and papers from the table to his bed to make room for the tray.

'Hannah, isn't it?' he said, when she came in. 'This is very nice of you.'

'You should have had some earlier, when you first came, only . . .' Hannah stopped, not knowing how to go on. She should not have said anything; he must know why no one had got round to making him any tea. 'Dinner's at seven, tonight.'

'You don't know what it is, do you?' Martin Carter said, hungrily.

Gavin Russell fell upon the teapot with such enthusiasm that he looked as if he might be about to suck the tea straight out of the spout.

'Stew,' Hannah said. 'We've just got it started. Can I get you anything else, Mr Carter?'

'Do call me Martin,' he said. 'And this is Gavin. Your little friend Dina kept calling me Martincarter as if it was all one word. Do you actually work here?' She could see that he was trying to discover if she could be much older than she looked.

'Oh no,' she said. 'I just help, in the holidays. I like coming here.'

'And what about Dina?' It was even harder to guess Dina's age, especially when she was adorned in her celebrity-hunting gear.

'She just hangs about.'

'I'm afraid we spoiled your day,' Martin said. 'I expect you had other things planned, you and Dina.'

Hannah could hardly admit that she spent most of her time planning ways of keeping Dina as far from West Stenning as possible.

'Dina's ever so pleased,' she said. 'You're her favourite actor.' She did not add that everyone was Dina's favourite actor, even people who appeared in soup commercials, dressed as turnips.

'Polly's not, though,' Martin said. 'I don't think I'm Polly's flavour of the month, at the moment.'

'Stop knocking nails into yourself, Mart,' Gavin Russell said, and walloped him across the shoulders. 'He's mortified,' he explained to Hannah. 'You should see *my* daughter.'

'Yes, but your daughter's in Chicago,' Martin said. He wouldn't be comforted.

'Tell them we'll be down when we've had this,' Gavin said, as Hannah moved towards the door. 'And thank you very much.'

She went back to the kitchen where George had just twisted the neck off a wine bottle while trying to pull out the cork. Polly was swabbing round his feet with a mop and the typewriter stuttered in the office. Things were getting back to normal.

At quarter to six George went off in the van to meet the course members at Ashford station, while those who had their own transport were beginning to arrive and park their cars in the yard. This was the signal for Hannah to leave, too, and George offered her a lift. They were just crossing the cattle grid when she saw Dina's bicycle leaning against the hedge, abandoned. Dina must have forgotten about it in the excitement of travelling with Martin Carter. They slung it into the Transit alongside Hannah's own bicycle and the two machines jostled and jangled together all the way up the hill and down into the village, playing strange duets when their bells collided.

Hannah thought that Dina might come out when she saw the Transit pull up at the gate, but no one opened the door. She left her own machine by the fence and wheeled Dina's up to the front door. There was an illuminated bell-push in the porch which chimed a row of soft notes when she pressed it. Mrs Swain came to the door and looked surprised to see Hannah there. It was the first time that Hannah had ever come calling for Dina and Mrs Swain thought Hannah was stuck-up because of it.

'Yes?' she said.

'I brought Dina's bike back,' Hannah said. 'She left it down at West Stenning.'

'Thank you,' said Mrs Swain, beginning to close the door.

'How's Julia?' Hannah said.

'On the phone,' Mrs Swain said, bitterly. 'She's already rung her mum. Now she's after her dad. She seems afraid they'll forget her if she's out of sight for five minutes. Chance would be a fine thing.'

Mum or Polly would have answered the phone, so Martin Carter had probably been left to unpack in peace. The door of the living-room opened behind Mrs Swain and Dina looked out.

'Oh, it's you.' She did not ask Hannah to come in, either.

'I brought your bike back,' Hannah said. 'You left it in the hedge.'

'You needn't have bothered,' Dina said. 'I was going to pick it up in the morning.'

'Tomorrow morning?'

'When I go down with Julie.'

'Julia.' Definitely not a Julie, as Dina would no doubt find out. 'You can't go down there tomorrow. The course has started.'

'Julie's going down. I'll have to show her the way.'

Mrs Swain went back into the kitchen. Hannah and Dina were left facing each other across the doorstep.

'She won't be allowed,' Hannah said. 'Not during a course.'

'She'll go down if she wants,' Dina said, and there was a look in her eye that Hannah had not seen before. 'And she'll get me her dad's autograph. *And* Gavin Russell's. You needn't bother.' She closed the door, muttering something, not even bothering to say goodbye properly. Hannah turned away.

The serial, *Decisions*, was on again this evening, a repeat of Monday's broadcast. Hannah had seen it already, but she watched again. Major Nevard was back in the army and already you could see that his men would die for him. They would probably have to, Hannah thought, sourly, this being a war. And there was an army lady, in ugly shoes and an even uglier haircut, who looked ready to follow him anywhere. Hannah, who had been hooked on Monday, no longer believed a word of it. Every time Major Nevard appeared she saw the grey-haired harassed man who leaned out of a window and hid his face in his hands. Major Nevard had no daughters.

Thursday, August 13th. Hi. Something really brilliant's happened. Hannah's furious. Martin Carter's daughter came down from Oxford with him and there wasn't anywhere to stay at West Stenning so she's staying here with us. I can't do much diary tonight as she'll be up in a minute. She's got the room next to mine and she'd hear me through the wall. She might think I was a nutcase, talking to myself. I wish I had a proper microphone so I could talk under the bedclothes. I can't get the radio in, the cord's not long enough. Next time we go to Ashford I'll get some batteries. Julie's downstairs phoning her mum. Her mum and dad are divorced. It's just like the play with Major Nevard. He's met this army lady and you can see what's going to happen. His leg isn't so bad this week. Here comes Julie. Perhaps we can tap messages on the wall. Byeeeee.

Chapter Eight

Karen was waiting for her O level results. These were not due for several weeks and in the meantime Karen behaved as if she were suffering from a debilitating disease from which she did not expect to recover. This involved getting up very late and spending an hour getting dressed, and another hour eating breakfast. Hannah knew from experience that it was unwise to wake Karen before she was ready to wake up by herself, so she got out of bed very quietly and did not open the curtains, searching for her clothes in the dark pink light that was all that filtered through. They were supposed to have half the room each, but Karen's belongings had gradually escaped from her side. Her make-up occupied the whole of the dressing-table top, her shoes were under Hannah's bed, Hannah's clothes were squeezed up into the very end of the wardrobe, elbowed aside by Karen's shirts and jackets that hung on Hannah's hangers. Karen's collection of earrings spread across the window sill and her pop posters covered all four walls, as well as the ceiling. The favourites were round and over Karen's own bed; when someone fell out of favour his picture was taken down and either thrown out or relegated to Hannah's side of the room. Every time she went in there, every morning when she opened her eyes on it, she thought of the little back bedroom at West Stenning, with the sloping ceiling and the diamond window panes.

Downstairs the kitchen was empty. Dad had already gone to his job at the mushroom farm, where he was foreman, and Mum was in the garden hanging some washing on the line, mostly Karen's curiously shaped garments; gloves without fingers, T-shirts without sleeves, tights without feet. Anyone who saw Karen's clothes without having seen Karen would imagine an incomplete person, lopped-off and full of holes. The door of the garden shed was open so Hannah could see that Tom's bicycle was missing. He was always first up and out of the house, to catch early birds.

Mum came back in while Hannah was making toast. Once the courses had begun her hours were shorter; she went to work in the afternoons only on Thurdays and Fridays and Hannah was banned from the house altogether although, like Tom, she could go where she liked in the grounds, so long as she kept well clear of aspiring writers or painters in the bushes. Musicians were easier to avoid; you could hear them. As Mum came in someone knocked at the front door.

'I'll go. You get on with your toast. Watch the grill,' Mum said, as if that last warning were necessary, although it was Karen who dozed between the headphones of her Walkman and woke to clouds of black smoke.

Mum came back after a moment. 'It's Dina. Wants to know if she can borrow your bike for Julie.'

'Julia,' Hannah said, automatically. 'Where are they going?'

'How should I know? For a ride, she said.' Mum did not suggest that Hannah dealt with Dina herself. Hannah could never get rid of Dina, and Mum could do it in a matter of seconds.

'I suppose so.' It occurred to Hannah that maybe Dina had more sense than she had given her credit for. If she took Julia for a bike ride it would keep them both away from West Stenning. Dina herself would be quite happy just to spend the day with the daughter of a famous actor even if they went nowhere more exciting than the local tip.

Mum went to deliver the message and after a moment Hannah saw Dina come into the back garden and go to the shed. She was wearing ordinary clothes, a good sign. When Dina re-emerged, wheeling Hannah's bicycle, Hannah leaned across the sink and knocked on the pane, meaning to wave, but Dina did not hear or, rather, pretended not to hear, although she was only a metre or two from the window. Clearly she did not want Hannah muscling in on her new friendship, but there was something almost furtive about the way she kept her head down, as if she had known that Hannah was at the window, even before she knocked on it.

Hannah stayed where she was, watching the back gate swing shut. Suppose they were not going for a bike ride at all or worse, for a ride that would take them through the village, on to the Challock Road and then straight down to West Stenning. If Julia said that this was where she wanted to go, Dina would never be the one to stop her. Hannah darted into the hall. Mum had gone upstairs. She opened the front door and looked to the left, across the crescent to Dina's house, but there was no sign of Dina, although even if she had ridden home she would scarcely have had time to reach her gate. Hannah ran down the path and into the road. In the other direction, towards the village, she could see two figures on bicycles, riding suspiciously quickly.

Her first thought was to go up and tell Mum; surely this didn't count as tale-bearing, but what would Mum do? Hannah had a feeling that if Dina and Julia went to West Stenning it would somehow turn out to be her fault. She would have to sort this out for herself and go down there, in spite of the unwritten law about courses; and she would have to go on foot. Dad's bicycle and Tom's were already in use, her own was with Dina and it would be very dangerous to ask to borrow Mum's. Karen had sold hers to help pay for the Walkman.

Even if she started now, and ran all the way, her route through Lord Sherlock's land and past Forstall Wood took far longer than a bicycle on the road. At least Mum did not know about this route.

There was a shout from indoors. Hannah raced back into the house, but she could smell burned toast before she was over the doorstep.

Tom, with his binoculars, drew a bead on the manor house. It filled the lenses, in its hollow, and dissolved as his eyes went out of focus. In its place he saw a great white maze of pre-cast concrete, winding, curving, turning back on itself in serpentine loops, crossed by bridges as intricate as the knotwork on the cross in the churchyard. He had spent days experimenting with configurations until he came up with what he regarded as the perfect blueprint.

The most impressive sight he had ever seen was a council estate near Gravesend where two sides of a valley swept down to a road, and on either side, as far as the eye could see, houses, roofs, chimney stacks. At night he lay in the dark piling street upon street, in terraces, along the flank of the downs from Maidstone to Folkestone; Stenning New Town. Unfortunately, West Stenning Manor would be swamped by this massive expansion, but he did not let that deter him; he had ideas about West Stenning. His notebook was filling with maps; field after field planted with rows of houses, blocks of flats, shopping precincts and schools; Hothfield Close, Forstall Crescent (the wood would have to go), Sherlock Square, Manor Avenue, Quarry Lane, Brook Street. The Fylde Brook itself was doomed to be diverted through a concrete pipe, but it could be let out at the end of Manor Avenue, to form an ornamental lake with seats round it and public toilets. The Pilgrim Leisure Centre would stand just about where the church was now; an ideal site although he was not certain if you were allowed to knock churches down.

Tom took everything into consideration and allowed himself the small indulgence of naming a block of flats after the architect: Fisk Tower.

By the time the cinders were cleared away and the smoke dispersed, it was nine o'clock. If Dina and Julia *had* been going to West Stenning, they would be there by now and Polly would be along at half past. Hannah looked out of the kitchen window and up the garden. There was no need for concealment now, in Dina's absence, and Mum never asked her where she was going when she climbed up the rubbish heap and over the fence. Mum was upstairs again, arguing with Karen about who had nicked the new box of tissues. Hannah had already been grilled about this and Tom wouldn't bother with tissues; he used his arm. Hannah left them snarling at each other and went up the garden, into the wasteland. The day was dry so far but fat waterlogged clouds hung over the downs. If a spiky tree so much as pricked one of those bulging swags the clouds would burst and deluge, turning the thin grass to slithering silk over the chalk, and beating flat Lord Sherlock's barley, down along the Challock Road.

Hannah ran up the headland of the wheatfield in the lee of the thorn hedge, and arrived at the footpath just in time to see George, on four legs again, trotting away from her in the direction of the woods. Hannah was glad to have missed him for once. If anything were amiss down at the manor she wanted to find out for herself rather than be told, by someone who would sound as if they expected her to do something about it. Tom would be a useful person to run into because he was sympathetic although he never did anything helpful. Tom took things as they came; he hadn't yet learned that sometimes you had to go after what you wanted, or take evasive action to avoid what you didn't want. He made no plans. Tom took it for granted that he should have the run of West Stenning, not realizing that he was allowed there because Hannah had asked permission, and that he was in no danger of losing his privileges because of Dina. Hannah doubted if he could be mobilized to defend their rights.

The downpour began as she came out of the wood and over the stile. Below she saw several little figures approaching the house at a scurry, course members who had been out looking for inspiration without their raincoats. They always reminded her of Pooh and Piglet looking for the Woozle, going round and round in circles, because they always ended up indoors, sitting at a table and chewing their biros, just like Hannah herself when she was told to write a story at school.

The sheep, who were quite clever about weather although not about anything else, were standing in the lee of the hornbeam thicket. Some had sat down resignedly and on the back of one was a round orange cushion; Ogmore, fast asleep. Ogmore could not tell the difference between a sheep and a hearthrug and never seemed to notice if he woke up in a different place from the one in which he'd gone to sleep.

Neither the Transit nor the yellow Volkswagen was in the yard, which meant that Polly had not yet arrived. Martin Carter's Morris was still up at Twining's the garage; there was nothing in the stable except two bicycles, her own and Dina's. Hannah felt too angry to be pleased that she had made the right guess; but where could they be? It was possible that they had seen her coming down through the pasture and were hiding somewhere about the place, somewhere wet, she hoped, under a leaky gutter and unable to come out in case she saw them. But Julia, she suspected, would be very pleased if she did see them, Julia who thought she could go where she liked. Hannah pressed herself against the wall of the outhouse, edged round it and then belted across the slippery sets to the side wall of the house, under the overhanging thatch.

Just round the corner was the grandly named Seminar Room, although it was only like a big living-room with easy chairs and sofas, where people sat around talking. She bent double and shuffled round until she was under the window sill. One of the casements was open for the overhang was wide enough to shelter it. She moved a little way from the wall and looked upwards and sideways, wrynecked. A broad back was blocking the casement, topped by another overhang of black thatch. 'Of course,' said a deep voice, 'it's quite different with radio. When you do a thirty-minute radio script they need thirty seconds, say, for the credits, and the remaining twenty-nine and a half minutes is up to you. You're responsible for everything . . .'

Gavin Russell was addressing the course members.

'Have you done any radio work?' a voice asked, and Hannah heard Martin Carter answer. His voice was much quieter than Gavin's, but very clear, his acting voice, not the one he had been using yesterday.

Hannah dared not raise her head to peer round Gavin's bulk, but she knew that course members met regularly with their tutors in the Seminar Room. This meant that the rest of the house would be empty; she could case the joint. Still stooping she scuttled along the wall and rose cautiously to look in at the dining-room window. The long table, where twenty-four people could sit in comfort, shone back at her from between two rows of chair backs. The chairs were empty. Hannah moved on, and rounded the corner.

It would have been like a game, had she been in the mood for games. At the west end of the house was a little side door that led into a passage. On one side was the broom cupboard, on the other the pantry with its big fridge freezer where Polly parked the food for the whole weekend. It was a good private place, a place Hannah would have chosen if she were hiding from someone. She glanced in at the boxes of fruit and vegetables, the terracotta bread-crock that looked like a funeral urn in a cemetery, the humming freezer; there was no one there, no signs of anyone having been there except for a mousetrap with no corpse in it, and this only meant that Tom had paid a very early morning call to spring it.

It was the only illicit thing he did, and so far he hadn't been caught. He did not mind Martha and Bertha catching mice because he knew about food chains, but he thought that mousetraps were cheating, although he would not have objected so much if George or Polly had eaten the mice themselves. As he always removed the cheese as well, people thought that West Stenning must harbour a special breed of very fly mice with lightning reflexes.

Hannah closed the door and looked in the broom cupboard. She did not really believe that Julia Carter would hide in a broom cupboard but she was leaving nothing to chance. It too was empty, dark and smelling like all broom cupboards, of dust and furniture polish.

The door at the end of the passage led into a small lobby known as the airlock, because you had to shut one door before you could open the other and get out again. On one side were the back stairs that led up to the landing, on the other, the door to the kitchen. Hannah put her ear to it and heard voices; quite high voices; children, not course members. She pressed her thumb gently to the latch and opened the door very quietly on Dina and Julia who were sitting at the table, calmly enjoying a late breakfast. Two coffee mugs steamed between them, the giant caterer's can of marmalade stood open with a knife stuck in it beside a newly unwrapped slab of butter, and Julia was sawing spongy doorsteps off a hacked-about loaf. Hannah opened the door wide and stormed in.

Dina jumped and blushed, scattering crumbs. Julia said, 'Look who's here,' without seeming to look at all, and went on cutting bread.

'Oh!' Dina said. 'Oh Hannah . . . oh . . .'

'Sit down,' Julia commanded, maddeningly self-possessed. 'Anyone'd think it was the Queen walked in. *She* thinks she is.'

Hannah could think of nothing to say to this except 'Who's she? The cat's mother?' which wouldn't do at all, so she said nothing. The door swung shut behind her, trapping them all together in a cage of light which came, she noticed, from the open door of the little kitchen refrigerator where breakfast things were kept; milk, butter, eggs and cartons of fruit juice. One of these cartons was also on the table, with its top carved off. Hannah moved round behind Julia and pushed the door shut.

'Don't you know better than to leave a fridge open?'

Dina started again. 'Oh Hannah, I'm sorry. Oh Hannah . . .'

'Oh be quiet,' Julia snapped. 'Anyone'd think it was *her* fridge. You don't own this place, you know,' she said, turning to Hannah for the first time.

'Who said I did?'

'Anyone'd think you did,' Julia said.

'I'm not supposed to be here at all, now the course has started,' Hannah said. 'None of us are. You'd better clear that lot up and get out before Polly comes. You've got five minutes.'

Dina leaped up again and made a twitchy grab for the marmalade can, overturning the fruit juice. Diving sideways to rescue the carton she elbowed one of the coffee mugs which slopped over, causing a mucky swamp of coffee and crumbs across the table-top.

'Oh, *stop* it,' Julia said. 'Anyone'd think there was a *law* about it. Who's Polly, when she's at home?'

'Mrs Ballard,' Hannah said. 'She's the course director; you met her yesterday. You'd *better* go before she gets here.'

'I don't care what she says. If my father says I can stay I shall.'

Hannah was willing to bet that Martin Carter had said no such thing. She wanted to say, 'Your father's a jellyfish and my mother thinks you need a good walloping,' but Julia hadn't finished.

'And Dina's my friend, so she can stay with me.'

Dina looked at Hannah, then at Julia, in a flat spin. She was no good at decisions. Julia looked at Dina and smiled slightly, and Hannah saw what was going on. Julia didn't care whether Dina stayed or not, but she had guessed how much Hannah would care, Hannah who had connived at and witnessed her defeat, yesterday. If Julia got nothing else out of her visit she was going to make sure that she put one across Hannah.

Dina was making half-hearted attempts to clear up the mess, dabbing a paper towel at the coffee swamp with one hand and trying to squash the plastic cap back on to the marmalade can with the other, unable to choose between the reflected glory of Julia's company and her longer – although not very long – friendship with Hannah. She too would enjoy getting one across Hannah, walking in and out of West Stenning when and as she felt like it, and Hannah unable to keep her away. She couldn't see ahead to the time when Julia went away again and Hannah would be free to take her revenge. Dina, Hannah thought pityingly, couldn't even see that Julia despised her already.

The cattle grid growled. This meant nothing to Julia, who was buttering another piece of bread – how did she stay so thin? – but Dina reacted like a hare that has heard gunfire.

Her ears did not quite prick but her eyes widened and she stood paralysed.

'That's Polly now,' Hannah said, as the Transit swept into the yard. It sounded bad-tempered, the snarl of tyres biting on newly wet dust and stones. '*Move.*'

But it was too late for them to move; they did not know where to move to, and if they went out of the kitchen door they would run into Polly whose brisk footsteps could even now be heard crossing the sets. Hannah moved instead. As Polly opened the kitchen door Hannah reached behind her, opened the door of the airlock and slipped round it.

'What's this then?' she heard Polly say, in a little furious voice, as she soundlessly lowered the latch. 'What, exactly, is this?'

For nearly a minute there was silence. Hannah could imagine Dina trying to answer, mouth dropping ever more open as the words piled up behind her teeth. Then Julia said sulkily, '*She* said it would be all right. Hannah did.'

'*Hannah?*'

'She said she comes here when she likes. She said it wouldn't matter.'

Dina said, 'Oh, *Julie* . . .'

As well she might. Hannah ground her teeth. Whatever Julia knew about Hannah she had learned from Dina. She wished she could see through the door for there was another silence, and she guessed that Julia and Dina had just turned round and noticed that she was no longer there.

'She was here just now,' Julia said. 'She was with us. Here.'

Polly shouted. 'Hannah!'

Either she could make a run for it, down the passage to the side door and away through the hornbeam thicket, or she could face it out in the kitchen. She went into the kitchen. Polly was still standing in the doorway and even from the far side of the room Hannah could see that she was shaking with anger. Looking at the mess on the table, it was easy to see why. One of the few rules at West Stenning was that people should clear up after themselves. None of the course members would have left the table in that state.

'Well?' Polly said. Hannah said nothing. 'Julia says you told her that she and Dina could come down here. You know perfectly well –'

'I never. I never said that,' Hannah shouted. 'I told them they shouldn't be here. I told them I don't come down here once courses start.'

'You're here now,' Polly said.

'I guessed they'd be here. I came specially, to tell them –'

'That's not what you said yesterday,' Julia muttered, but she was looking less sure of herself. She had underestimated Polly.

Polly could see that someone was lying but she was too furious to stop and work out who it might be. She pointed to the door. 'Out! Both of you. Go home at once. Leave that coffee, Julia.'

'My father . . .' Julia began.

'If I see you here once more, your father will be taking you straight back to London,' Polly said. She threw open the kitchen door and held it back with her arm until Julia had stalked out, followed by Dina who looked as if she might cry. Hannah hoped that she *was* crying and that she would now see what hanging around with Julia could entail.

'You clear up,' Polly said, letting the door bang shut and nearly cutting off Bertha's head as she ran in from the rain. Hannah advanced towards the table.

'I never said she could come here. Honestly, Polly, I never would.'

'And when you've finished,' Polly went on, icily, 'you can clear off too. Don't ever let me catch you down here again.'

'Never?' Hannah said. She felt that same blank helplessness that came over her at school when there was trouble threatening; the feeling that hit her at the moment she realized that there was no way out of it.

'During a course,' Polly growled. She was softening, her rage was easing up. Hannah, in a rush of relief, had time to wonder what was the matter with Polly. Polly had a temper, she knew, but she'd never let rip like this before. George wouldn't have stood a chance against such fury. She'd have bitten him in half and gnawed his bones.

Polly went through to the office, her sandals slapping on the flagstones. Clearing up did not take so very long and Hannah felt sourly pleased to see that in spite of all their preparations, Julia and Dina had scarcely had time to eat anything. She put the milk and juice back in the fridge and returned the loaf to the pantry bread-crock. As she came back into the kitchen she heard voices and footsteps from the direction of the Seminar Room. The meeting had broken up and was heading for the kitchen to make coffee. Hannah frantically swiped the dishcloth over the sticky table and dived for the airlock, feeling like one of those domestic hobgoblins she had read about in fairy tales, who dare not be seen by the householder, and cursing Julia all over again for turning her into an interloper.

Coming out of the side door she turned left, to the back of the house, but the rain had stopped and several of the course members had come out on to the little patch of grass that was able to call itself a lawn because George mowed it once a fortnight. Gavin Russell strode among them, exactly the shape of Humpty Dumpty in *Alice Through the Looking Glass*, except that Humpty had worn his face on the front of his body while Gavin's was in the usual place, on top of his neck.

Hannah ducked back into the doorway; she did not want to walk among the course members and if Polly saw her doing it there would be more trouble. She would have to go the other way, over the cattle grid and up the hill to the village. Once over the grid she would be back in bounds, and there she paused to look back, down into the yard. Martin Carter came round the corner and crossed to the stable. He was too far away for her to see how he looked, but from the way he walked she could guess how he felt, and now she knew how Dina felt, too; banned from Paradise, on the far side of the cattle grid.

And Julia had her bicycle. She would have to walk home.

Chapter Nine

Coming round the corner by the church Hannah saw Mum, further down the street and cycling from the opposite direction. It was far too early for her to be coming to work on a Friday; she must be going to the shops, but if she saw Hannah she would guess where she had been. Hannah had been hoping devoutly that when Mum did get to work, Polly would be too tactful to tell her what had happened this morning; not so tactful that she wouldn't mention Julia's misdemeanour, just tactful enough to leave out the fact that Hannah had been there too. Certainly she did not want to meet Mum just yet. She dodged sideways under the lich-gate and into the churchyard, where she hid behind a table-tomb, beside the path.

From there she should be able to see which shop Mum went into, but to her dismay, Mum kept coming. Either she *was* going to the manor, out of hours, or she was going to see someone. Hannah bobbed down again as Mum's head and shoulders glided into view above the wall of the churchyard. But then they stopped and jolted in a way that suggested that Mum had got off the bicycle, probably to speak to someone, someone on the far side of the road whom Hannah could not see.

She wondered how long she would have to stay in hiding. Mum wouldn't mind her being in the graveyard but she would be certain to say, as she always did, 'You haven't been down to West Stenning, have you?' If Hannah said no, and Polly then tattled, there would be the biggest row on record. She would never be allowed to go there again. Mum showed no signs of moving on; it was clearly going to be a day for dodging and ducking.

Still crouching, Hannah sidled from the shelter of her tomb to the next, the sheer sides of the Sherlocks' granite box. This housed the vault of a low-down, outdoor class of Sherlock. The top brass had their tombs in the church, up near the altar, although it was some years since Sherlocks of any kind had been buried at Stenning. They probably had themselves democratically cremated these days, in any case.

Slipping from grave to grave and constantly looking over her shoulder at Mum's wagging, chatting head, Hannah worked her way round to the west end of the church, safely out of sight at last; but when she raised her head she found herself looking through the spokes of a bicycle wheel. The bicycle was propped against a headstone. Hannah looked more closely; it was her own bicycle. Dina's machine was a little way off, leaning on a buttress. Hannah threw herself flat again and listened for voices. At first she heard only Mum and whoever it was Mum was talking to; then there was another voice, much closer, round by the water tank on the south side of the church.

'Anyone'd think *I* didn't count.'

No prizes offered for guessing who *that* was.

'You're not sorry you came, are you?' Dina said, plaintively.

'*She'll* be sorry,' Julia said. Who, Hannah wondered. Polly? Me?

'She's got this boyfriend called Michael Atkins. *I*'m in the way.'

Not me, then, thought Hannah. Not Polly, either. It would be splendid to leap round the edge of the buttress. Dina would probably faint with fright but Julia . . . no. Julia would ruin it. Julia would say, 'Huh. Anyone'd think you were Wonderwoman.' Then she had a better idea.

She slipped round the west end of the church again and looked over the top of the Sherlock tomb. Mum was just moving off, heading for the Hothfield Road. She had friends down there, just past the police house; that should keep her busy for a bit. Noiselessly Hannah took her bicycle from where it stood and wheeled it across the grass towards the road, avoiding the gravel path until she reached the lichgate. It was a good move, she thought. To have taken Dina's machine would be nicking; nicking her own was just repossession. She would have liked to hide the bicycle and creep back to hear what happened when Dina discovered the loss, but the graveyard was so tidy there was nowhere to hide it, and if Dina found it too quickly she would realize that someone was playing games. As she was mounting it Tom came coasting round the corner, from the quarry, no doubt. Tom was a maniac. How could any sane person spend so much time just watching for birds?

'Been grave robbing?' Tom said, as he overtook her.

'Bike robbing,' Hannah said.

'What d'you mean, bike robbing? That *is* your bike.'

'I lent it to Dina,' Hannah said. 'You know that girl I was telling you about – Julia Carter, staying at Dina's?'

'I saw her, didn't I?' Tom said. He mimed accurately. 'All mouth.'

'Dina borrowed my bike this morning,' Hannah said, as they rode through the village. 'She borrowed it for Julia – and do you know where they went?'

'There's a dead sheep in the quarry,' Tom said. 'It must have fallen off the top. Do you think I should tell someone?'

Hannah persevered. 'They went down to the manor and had *breakfast*. Polly went mad.'

'What were you doing there, then?' Tom asked.

'How do you know I was there?'

'I saw you come down. I was hiding behind a sheep,' Tom said. 'I won't tell Mum.'

'I just hope Polly doesn't. I guessed they'd gone down there so I went to warn them off, but Polly came before they went. If she lets on to Mum I was there I don't know what'll happen.'

'You'll get banned,' Tom said, cheerfully. He couldn't see that it mattered one way or the other. Like Polly, he thought that there were plenty of other places to play. 'Why don't you tell her first. She likes it if we own up.'

'But I didn't do anything,' Hannah said. 'Anyway, she'll still say it was my fault.'

'Is that why you nicked your bike back? To get at Dina?'

'To scare her,' Hannah said. 'She'll think it's been properly stolen.'

'She'll go to the police, then,' Tom said.

'She'd look for it first.'

'Yes, but she won't find it,' Tom pointed out. They had reached home. He did a two-wheel drift to the gate and leaped off the bicycle, leaving the wheels spinning. 'She'll go down the police house and report it. That'll make her feel daft, when she finds you've had it all the time.' He nodded approvingly, evidently deciding that it was a good idea after all. Hannah was thinking just the opposite.

'I'll get in an awful row if she does. With the police and that.'

'Say it was a joke.'

'It was . . . sort of. That won't make any difference.' Hannah began to turn the bicycle round in a wobbling, uncertain semicircle. 'I'd better take it back.'

'Don't suppose they'll have noticed it's gone, yet,' Tom said. 'Bet they were yakking nineteen to the dozen anyway. You could have pinched the shoes off their feet and they wouldn't have seen you.'

Hannah dismounted at the lich-gate and wheeled the machine over the muffling turf, between the graves, following the line of the tyres that she had made earlier, but when she reached the west end of the church she stopped. Dina's bicycle had disappeared too.

Hannah threw down hers and ran round to the water tank. It was a big galvanized iron cube that collected all the rainwater that ran off the lead roof of the church. The water was green and usually had mosquito larvae and dead moths, delicate as flower petals, floating on top. Because this was the end-of-the-garden part of the churchyard, where the wheelbarrow and watering cans stood, the grass was allowed to grow long and weedy. Behind the water tank was a flattened patch where Dina and Julia had been sitting; some scraps of paper and tin foil off a packet of Polos lay about. Julia's evil influence again; Dina wouldn't drop litter, especially not in a churchyard. She did go to church sometimes and was very superstitious about walking on the tombstones set in the floor of the aisle.

Hannah leaned on the water tank, looking at her green reflection, and did some quick thinking. In the ten minutes since she had taken the bicycle Dina and Julia had vanished. Either they had gone down the Hothfield Road, in which case she could easily catch them up, or they had gone back to West Stenning. Why should they go to West Stenning – particularly after what had happened there this morning? Why should they go down the Hothfield Road? Hannah looked up with a jerk that made the green mirror quake and sent the mosquito larvae wriggling fast to the bottom. Above the churchyard wall, between two yews, she could see the roof of a house on the Hothfield Road, and a part of its front wall. There was a plaque set in that wall, between the two upstairs windows, that read KENT COUNTY CONSTABULARY. The constabulary in East Stenning was David Holdstock and Hannah was on friendly terms with him. Rodney and Alison Holdstock went to her school and when she saw them all together he was just Mr Holdstock, Alison and Rodney's dad. But when he was at work he was Sergeant Holdstock; he would be Sergeant Holdstock right now.

Hannah left the tank and crept across the grass, keeping one of the yews between her and the house until she was up against the wall. She raised her head and looked over. Except for its plaque and blue front door the police house looked like any other house, with an ordinary front garden and a concrete path to the gate. Coming *down* the path, from the door, were Dina and Julia. Dina's bicycle was propped against the fence. Hannah stood and gazed. She knew what they had been doing. They had been to report a theft. Trust Dina to panic and ruin everything.

She had two options; to call them and explain what she had done or to wait and see what happened next. Explaining what she had done would involve further explanations with Sergeant Holdstock, and while she was wondering about that Dina and Julia disappeared round the bend in the road. Hannah left her post and ran, stooping below the wall, to the lich-gate where she waited for them to reappear; but they did not reappear and after a few moments she realized that they must have taken the Challock Road. The Challock Road led to Challock – and to West Stenning; to *West Stenning.*

All thoughts of owning up evaporated. If Sergeant Holdstock accused her of wasting police time she would plead that she had a perfect right to take her own bicycle, that she had thought Dina had abandoned it – Dina was like that, she would say. Let Dina stew in her own juice for a bit longer. What Hannah must do now was hide the evidence.

Tom was in luck. Karen had not been down to the kitchen, he could hear her thumping about overhead, and the provisions that Mum had left in the refrigerator were still untouched. It was not yet eleven, but Tom knew that a pre-emptive strike was the only way of making certain that he got any lunch worth speaking of. He assembled a heap of spring onions, radishes and cheese, lightly garnished with two slices of bread, filled his water bottle with pineapple and passionfruit squash, liberated a couple of oranges from the living-room fruit bowl and, stowing it all about his person, sailed off again on his bicycle.

By this time Hannah had disappeared, but Tom had already forgotten about Hannah and her problems. As he passed the church and turned right towards West Stenning his mind was on more rewarding things. The Stour Valley Interchange had one particular advantage over Spaghetti Junction; alongside every carriageway and sliproad ran an independent cycle track, quite separate from the traffic lanes, each requiring its own flyovers and underpasses and adding gloriously to the complexities of the system. The beleaguered inhabitants of Stenning New Town would be able to reach Ashford or Faversham or Canterbury – or Paris – without ever encountering a juggernaut. He had read somewhere that in the West Country, which he imagined to be somewhere to the left of Maidstone, special sections of the railway tracks had been made safe for badgers to cross. Apparently badgers always crossed the railway at the same place, and had been electrocuting themselves, until someone had come up with the idea of marking those places and breaking the current to let the badgers through. There were no badgers on the downs, so far as he knew, but he was considering a similar system for hedgehogs, perhaps diverting them into a large concrete pipe which would then convey them to safety across the valley over a series of hedgehog-sized viaducts. Almost without meaning to he had landed himself with a whole new network to devise, cutting across, over and under the existing motorways and cycle tracks; the Hedgehog Line. Joyfully he stood on his pedals and charged the hill.

He saw the obstruction in the road just in time to take evasive action and slewed to a halt. The obstruction was

Dina Swain and Julia Carter, and yet another bicycle, wrangling on the crown of the lane. Tom's usual method of dealing with other people's troubles was to smile pleasantly and pass by on the other side, but before he could move off Dina's hand shot out and gripped his handlebars.

'Hallo,' Tom said, politicly, when he saw there was no escape.

'Have you seen Hannah?'

'Not up here,' he said, truthfully.

'Have you seen Hannah's bike?'

'I saw it earlier,' Tom said. He waited until Dina began to look relieved and then said, to Julia, 'You were riding it.'

'I don't mean then,' Dina shouted. 'I mean just now.'

Tom, looking over Dina's shoulder, saw at the foot of the hill Hannah running across the churchyard.

'I saw Hannah just now,' he said.

'Did she have the bike?'

'She had *a* bike,' Tom said, 'but it couldn't have been hers. You've got it.'

'I haven't got it!' Dina screamed. 'Someone's nicked it.'

'Anyone'd think it was *worth* stealing,' Julia said. 'Who'd want that heap of scrap iron?'

'Ssssh,' Dina hissed. 'That's her brother.'

'I don't care whose brother it is. Anyone'd think –'

'I expect she went down to West Stenning,' Tom said.

'Was she going that way?'

'She wasn't when I saw her,' Tom said, 'but she might have, since. She likes it down there.' He gave them a wide, innocent grin.

'Are you going down there?' Dina said.

'I'm going over the quarry,' Tom said, changing his plans rapidly. The quarry was as good a place as any from which to launch the Hedgehog Line. 'Why don't you go down?' he asked.

'Mrs Ballard said we weren't to,' Dina said, blushing.

The mention of this prohibition acted like strong drink upon Julia.

'Anyone'd think she owned the place. She can't stop you.'

'She can. And she'd blame Hannah,' Dina said.

'Good. Let's go on down there.'

Dina shook her head, miserably. 'I'm not going there again. Mrs Ballard'll be there.'

'I don't care,' Julia retorted, predictably. 'And I don't care what you do.'

'I've got to look for the bike,' Dina said.

'I'm going to find Daddy.' She looked sidelong at Dina. 'Don't you want to come?'

'Can't.'

'I don't care if you come or not. I just thought you thought he was so marvellous.' Julia mounted Dina's bicycle, without asking Dina's permission, and freewheeled down towards West Stenning without so much as a glance at the gatehouse, as she passed it.

'Don't tell her,' Dina said, to Tom.

'Tell who? What?' Tom flirted his eyelashes like the dear little boy so many people thought he was.

'Don't tell Hannah I've lost her bike.'

'I thought you said someone had stolen it.'

'I don't know . . . they must have.'

'Suppose she asks?'

'Just say you don't know. I mean, you don't *know*, do you?' Dina was much too honest to make Tom lie on her behalf. 'Someone might just be mucking about. That's what the police said.'

'The police?'

'I've reported it,' Dina said. Tom's poker face stood him in good stead.

'That's all right then,' he remarked, and began wheeling his machine in the direction of the quarry. For about thirty seconds he wondered if taking your own property counted as stealing and if so, had Hannah committed a crime? But then he remembered the more pleasurable business of the Hedgehog Line and thoughts of criminal proceedings went right out of his head.

Dina watched him out of sight before turning to look at the entrance to West Stenning. On the right-hand side of the bend was a wide iron gate that stood always open, next to the little gatehouse where George and Polly Ballard lived. Presumably Polly was not around or she would have come out and stood in that gateway defending the track to the manor like the angel with a fiery sword who barred the gate of Paradise. It was possible that she had gone into Ashford, but more likely that she was down at the manor. It was a risk that Dina was not prepared to take, even for the sake of seeing Martin Carter.

A few seconds later she decided that sometimes you did get rewarded for being good. As she turned her steps back towards the village, round the corner, from the direction of the pub, came Gavin Russell and Martin Carter.

When they saw her they waved, just like real people.

'Have you lost Julia?' Martin Carter said.

'Oh no,' Dina stammered, visualizing herself in even more trouble for losing not only Hannah's bicycle but Martin Carter's daughter too. She pointed. 'She went down to West Stenning. She thought you'd be there.'

Julia's father and Gavin Russell looked at each other.

'Tell her to go back to the village if you see her,' Martin Carter muttered. 'I'll be round at teatime, like I said.'

'Anything you say, Major!' said Gavin Russell and saluted, with a lot of wheeling and stamping. Martin Carter punched his head, but in a friendly way, and Gavin Russell marched away whistling the theme music from *Decisions*. Dina was left with Martin Carter who was making some decisions of his own.

'Where does that path go?'

'Forstall Wood, but most of it's private.'

'What about that one?' He looked at the leafy depression among the trees, more like a ditch than a footpath, where Tom had earlier gone.

'That goes to the quarry.'

'Ah; I like quarries,' Martin Carter said, unconvincingly. He raised his hand to Dina and set off downhill between the coppiced chestnut trunks.

Dina watched him, as she had watched Tom, before resuming her trek to the village. Major Nevard would never hide from his own daughter although last week he had been hiding from his wife.

Hannah was still lurking by the lich-gate when she heard urgent footsteps and saw Dina go by at a run, heading homeward. Suddenly things looked simple. All she had to do was conceal the bicycle in a place where Dina would never think of looking and then, perhaps tomorrow, when Dina had worked up a good head of steam, find it herself and descend righteously upon Dina to demand explanations. She guessed that if Dina were alone Julia must have gone to West Stenning, and since Julia seemed to have Dina's bicycle, she had no doubt already arrived. But that was no excuse for hanging about. Hannah collected her bicycle from where it lay among the gravestones, wheeled it out of the churchyard and began to run with it up the steep slope of the Challock Road. Running was quicker than pedalling on that gradient, and on foot she would be better placed to take cover among the trees if she did meet anyone.

The road was empty. The only real hazard was the gatehouse and as it rose into view over the hump in the road Hannah saw that all the windows were closed, which meant that neither George nor Polly was at home. Hannah turned sharply right on to the footpath that ran through Forstall Wood, as she heard a car changing gear on the road ahead of her. It might be a harmless motorist on the Challock Road; on the other hand it might be a Ballard, coming up from the manor. Hannah put on such a spurt that she was hidden among the trees before she had a chance to look back and see which it was.

The footpath was not much used except by George, when he was running. Hannah toiled upwards, skidding on the damp beech leaves and snagged by brambles, until she reached the wire fence that marked Lord Sherlock's part of the woods. The path swerved to the left here, and Hannah followed it, still moving upwards until she came to a place where the undergrowth on the far side of the fence thinned out. She lifted the machine with one mighty swipe and swung it over the topmost strand of the wire, only just in time, for from further up the hill came the hefty chuff-chuff of rubber-soled trainers on deep leaves, and round the bend came George, head bent, elbows pumping.

Hannah did not wait to see how many legs he had today. She dived between the two middle strands of wire, landing partly, painfully, on the handlebars of the bicycle and partly, even more painfully, among nettles, old tough summer nettles, with savage stings.

It was unlikely that George could have seen her. He was gazing at something in his right hand, probably a stop-watch, but it would have been a risk she could not take. George was not the kind of person you could let in on this particular kind of secret; not on any kind of secret, come to that.

Hannah picked herself up. There was a round evil bruise coming on the inside of her thigh, just above the knee, where the left handlegrip had stabbed her, and the skin of her right arm was bubbling with nettle stings. Muttering and swearing she plucked the bicycle out of the brambles and set off uphill again, into the wood.

This was now Sherlock's Wood, the place where she never went. The trees stood taller here, straighter; private and haughty, *noble* trees; a better class of tree altogether than the ones that grew lower down on the public slope. It was darker, the undergrowth lusher, but apart from that there seemed to be no good reason for fencing it off except that it *did* belong to Lord Sherlock and he no doubt liked to prove it.

There were no paths; the terrain was foreign but Hannah knew that so long as she kept moving upwards she would eventually come to the hedge that flanked the headland of Lord Sherlock's wheatfield, and then she would know exactly where she was. Near the place where the hedge met the footpath was a glade that in May was thick with blue-bells, and circled by holly bushes. She had often eyed it wistfully over the hedge, especially in winter, when the holly was gemmed with berries. If she hid the bicycle there she would have no trouble finding it again when she needed it, and no one else would find it first.

Chapter Ten

Tom met Martin Carter unexpectedly in the quarry. He had just set up the tripod of fencing stakes and secured his binoculars to the apex, when he heard clumsy footfalls in the bushes. Assuming that it was a wandering course member he went on with what he was doing, since such people usually backed off rapidly when they stumbled across him. They were looking for inspiration, not children. When he saw who it was, he waved.

'Hallo, Mr Carter.'

Martin Carter, who was disengaging his jacket from a thorn bush, looked up nervously.

'Oh . . . it's Tom, isn't it? Am I disturbing you?'

Tom was not used to people apologizing if they disturbed him.

'Oh no, Mr Carter. Come in.'

Martin Carter walked into the clearing at the foot of

the chalk face. 'Do call me Martin. Are you bird-watching?'

Tom, making final adjustments to the binoculars, frowned disapprovingly. He thought it was rude to call grown-ups by their first names.

'I'm planning a bypass.'

'I see. Is that your theodolite?'

'That's right.' Tom trained the binoculars on the quarry face. 'We'll have to blast right through here.'

'What are you bypassing?'

'The housing estates.'

Martin Carter looked all round at the bushes, the chalk boulders, the grazing sheep outlined against the sky. 'Housing estates? Where? On the other side of the hill?'

'They haven't been built, yet.' Tom motioned him to sit down, which he did, on a boulder, and showed him the notebooks, and the maps.

'You're planning to tear down West Stenning Manor and put up houses?'

'A new town,' Tom corrected him. 'We wouldn't have to demolish the house. It could become a restaurant or something. But you wouldn't want the heavy traffic to go through the middle, would you?'

'I don't think I should,' Martin Carter said. 'I didn't know you had much heavy traffic up here.'

'We shall when they build the Channel Tunnel,' Tom said, dreamily. 'Juggernauts; sixteen-wheel rigs.' He turned back a page or two and displayed the flyover. 'This'll join the M2 and the A20 – it'll all be on viaducts across the valley but we'll need a cutting here, and there could be a bridge going across with motorway services on it, and sliproads coming down the sides, see? And rich people who didn't want to eat on the bridge could go down to the Manor Restaurant and have proper food.'

'What's going to happen to the writers and painters?'

'They'll be rehoused,' Tom said. 'Mr and Mrs Ballard can stay on at the restaurant and cook, or something.'

'I'm sure they'll be relieved to hear it,' Martin Carter said. 'But don't you think this place is rather nice as it is? I mean, don't you think that building a three-lane motorway and interchange system will spoil the view? A bit,' he added lamely, seeing that Tom looked unconvinced.

'But that's what happens,' Tom said. 'Motorways and things. You were an architect in that play at Christmas, weren't you?'

'That was about building a shopping centre in Greater Manchester, not a freeway through the North Downs.'

'They said you were a ruthless interpreter,' Tom said.

'Entrepreneur. That wasn't me, it was the part I was playing. I'm an actor, not an architect. Do I look ruthless?'

Tom surveyed him through the binoculars.

'No-o-o-o. That bit, where you're sitting, will be the central reservation. I'll call this Carter's Gap, if you like. Carter's Gap Services Area,' he said, and noted it down on the plan.

Friday, August 14th. Something awful's happened. Julie's still here. I don't mean it's awful that Julie's still here only I don't think I like her much, but something really bad.

Happened, I mean.

We went down to West Stenning this morning. I said we weren't allowed to but Julie said it would be all right because of her dad being there so I borrowed Hannah's bike for Julie to ride. I didn't tell Mrs Fisk why I wanted it. We went down early and there wasn't anybody about except the cats. One of them is deaf, the one called Bertha. She shouts a lot like deaf people do. Julie said we'd go and see her dad so we went up to the flat place over the garage and knocked. Martin Carter wasn't there but his friend was, the fat one with the beard. He said Julie's dad was with a student and we'd better go home because we weren't supposed to be there just like I said. And then he shut the door but Julie wouldn't come away, she said we could go and have breakfast in the kitchen and I said we shouldn't because of what her dad's friend had said but she said her dad said it would be all right. I don't think he did say that because Mrs Ballard came and said we mustn't so we went back to the village.

We got some Polos and went and sat in the churchyard round the back by the water tank and Julie told me all about where she lives in London, it's called Putney. She said she'd hate to live in Stenning because there's nobody here. There are a lot of people here but I know what she means. There's nobody interesting that's why I like going down to West Stenning. I don't really have any friends here and I've lived here since I was little.

Julie's dad's serial was on again last night. I think it's brilliant but Julie said it couldn't be or they wouldn't put it on in the summer.

While we were round by the church someone came and stole Hannah's bike. I haven't told her yet. She hasn't asked for it back yet. I don't know what I'll say when she does. I told the police. Sergeant Holdstock said someone was just mucking about probably, but he wrote it all down.

Mrs Ballard was horrible to me and Julie this morning. I don't want to go there again. Someone's coming. Bye.

Karen had fallen into bed last night without bothering to draw the curtains properly, so on Saturday morning Hannah was wakened for once by a shaft of sunlight, that fell across her pillow. She lay for a while, watching the dust spinning in it and working out what day it was.

Saturday: no chance of going down to West Stenning on a Saturday.

Then she remembered that yesterday had been Friday, and remembered what had happened. She changed gear and started wondering if Dina were awake yet at the other end of the crescent. Perhaps Dina had been awake all night, worrying about the bicycle; she ought to have been. Serve her right, for borrowing it under false pretences, falsely pretending that she and Julia were going for a ride and then sneaking down to West Stenning behind Hannah's back.

Mind you, Hannah thought, discovering that she did not feel as gleeful as she had expected to, that had almost certainly been Julia's idea, not Dina's. But Dina shouldn't have been such a drip as to let Julia order her about. She only did it because of Julia's dad, and look at *him*.

She slid quietly out of bed, for fear of waking Karen who would snarl and throw something, and looked out between the curtains. It was going to be a hot day; if the weather held they would all go to the coast tomorrow. A blue haze hung between her and the crest of trees on the downs, Lord Sherlock's trees, in the wood where the holly grove stood secretly guarding the bicycle.

Later on she would nip up through the wasteland and fetch it back down to the Challock Road, pretend that she had found it and go and set Dina's mind at rest, but no. Dina had not yet confessed. Hannah hardened her heart. Let Dina wait till after lunch, when the Fisks had been to Ashford for the weekend shopping. Let her wait.

At Number Ten, Pilgrims' Close, Julia was consulting her

diary. Today was one of her anniversaries; MMMAD; Mummy Met Michael Atkins Day. In fact she could not be sure that this was the case. It was the day that Mummy had *told* her that she had met Michael Atkins. It could have been going on for a long while before that, Julia told herself darkly, months and months. Julia had nothing at all against Michael Atkins himself; she liked him very much and if the worst came to the worst he would no doubt make a very good stepfather, especially as he had no children, but if he and Mummy got married . . . At least she ought to be consulted. Maybe after her dramatic flight on Thursday they would realize how desperately she minded. Julia tried to mind desperately.

Through the wall she could hear Dina Swain talking to herself and crying.

Dina Swain is retarded, Julia wrote in her diary. *I don't see why I should have to stay here. I want to be with Daddy only Mrs Ballard won't let me. I HATE HER. I wish I was dead. No one cares where I am.*

She could leave it open on the dressing-table when she went out. Mrs Swain looked just the kind of mother who would read a person's private diary.

Tom, who had already been up for a couple of hours, was conducting a funeral. One of the West Stenning mousetraps had, in spite of his precautions, finally claimed a victim. Standing by the grave, head bent, he intoned a few mournful words over the corpse, in the high-pitched nasal bleat that the Reverend Ascott used in church and which had impressed Tom enormously at last year's carol service, because it seemed to have no connection at all with human speech. He was used to singing songs to Jesus at school but they sang them in English: since Christmas he had come to the vague conclusion that God was foreign and probably didn't understand half of what was said to him.

'Eeeeenernameovverfaaaaaaaah, eeesuhuhuh, eeeeyolygo-o-ose,' Tom groaned, piously, and cast in a handful of earth. Then he sealed the tomb with a grubbed-up clump of bluebell bulbs and stood back. His elbow connected with a sharp object and there was a jangling crash behind him as something fell out of the holly bush.

Tom jumped. He spent a lot of time in the grove at the top of Sherlock's Wood, partly because he had taken to using it as a cemetery for the deceased hedgehogs which he scraped off the roads, but originally because it was from here that his motorway would begin its downward sweep towards the A20. His own house lay directly in its path but he knew that you could not afford to be sentimental where progress was concerned.

However, so far as he knew, no one else ever came near the grove, so he was fairly amazed, by his standards, when he saw that what had fallen out of the holly bush was his sister's bicycle.

Tut-tutting old-maidishly because it had crushed some tender plants, he picked it up and propped it back against the holly bush where it sagged and settled in. He was about to leave it, having made sure that it was secure, when it occurred to him to wonder what it was doing there. The last time he had seen it, Hannah had been riding it, on her way to replace it in the churchyard from where she had removed it, before Dina discovered that it was missing. Tom paused to consider, which was rare for him; he did most of his thinking on his feet. Either Dina had recovered the bicycle and hidden it here for some sinister purpose, or Julia Carter had been riding it and abandoned it because that was the kind of thing she would do with other people's property.

A third possibility struck him, that this time it really had been nicked, but why? It was not the kind of bicycle an honest-to-goodness thief would look twice at. It had been third-hand when Hannah got it. And then, again, who would bring a bicycle up here for any reason, pushing it all the way, humping it over stiles and fences? He stowed his own down at the junction of the footpath and the Challock Road when he came up here. It was for this eminently sensible reason that he left the bicycle where it was when he burrowed through the hedge, climbed the stile and ran down the pasture to the manor. By the time he arrived he had forgotten about it.

Hannah and Mum were going through the Saturday morning routine. They were word perfect.

'Why can't Karen go?'

'She isn't up yet. You know that.'

'Why isn't she up? She's never up.'

'Well *you're* up, so stop arguing.'

'I hate going to Sainsbury's. Why don't you *make* her get up?'

'Don't tell me what to do.'

'I'm not telling you what to do, I'm just asking . . .'

'You're not asking, you're whining. I can't stand people who –'

'Why can't Tom go? Tom never has to do anything.'

'Tom's too young to be any help. He just gets in the way.'

'Well, he always will if he never gets any practice in, won't he? Why don't you –?'

'Why, why, why. Why don't you do as you're told for

once without arguing? You're quick enough to help if Polly Ballard wants something done.'

At the mention of Polly, Hannah shut up.

The dialogue always ended with Dad hooting impatiently from the road outside.

'Oh shut up,' Mum said, as she invariably did when she heard the horn. 'Go out and tell him I'm just coming.' She was putting the milk money in an envelope to leave on the doorstep under a bottle, because Karen would not hear the milkman knock, nor come down to pay him if she did. Hannah ran down the path but Dad had lit a cigarette and was reading the newspaper, propped against the steering wheel, because he knew from experience that he would have a long while to wait. Without meaning to, Hannah glanced along the crescent. Most of the neighbours were doing what the Fisks were doing, preparing for the weekly shopping expedition to Ashford, but Mr Swain often worked on Saturdays and there was no car waiting outside the Swains' house. Outside the house was Dina, looking thin and still as if she were hoping to be taken for a gatepost.

Hannah tried to sound natural. She waved. 'Dina!'

If Dina said anything she was too far away and speaking too softly for Hannah to hear what it was. She flapped a hand at Dad, *hang on a minute*, although clearly Dad was going nowhere yet, and ran along the pavement. As she came close she saw that Dina looked so green and miserable that she almost called out, 'Hey, Dina, I've found it,' before she remembered that she was not yet supposed to know that it was missing. And then Dina mumbled, 'You don't want your bike back yet, do you?'

'Why?' Hannah felt her heart hardening all over again.

'Well, me and Julie'll probably go out somewhere,' Dina

said, looking over Hannah's shoulder at nothing in particular. 'I mean, you're going into Ashford. You won't need it yet, will you?'

'You think you can find it before lunchtime?' Hannah thought. She said, 'You're not going to West Stenning, *are you?*'

'Oh no.' Able to tell the truth again, Dina looked Hannah in the eye at last. 'I thought we might go up Challock a bit, or something.'

'OK.' Hannah began to walk away. 'I want it back by tonight, though.' She paused. 'Julia's not gone to West Stenning, has she?'

'I don't know where she is.' Dina blinked and bit her lip. 'She doesn't take any notice of what I say. She took *my* bike.'

Hannah spun round. '*Why?*'

'Oh . . .' Dina realized what she had said. 'Oh, she thinks it's better'n yours.'

There was no doubt at all that Dina's bicycle was better than Hannah's. It was twenty years younger for a start. This did not excuse Dina's tactlessness. Hannah gave her a last grim smile. 'Tonight, then,' she said, and did not look back again as she ran along the crescent to where Mum was waving impatiently by the car.

Tom had left his bicycle leaning against the wall of the gatehouse, and as he came cantering up the track from the manor he saw that there was another machine beside it, Dina's; but Dina was not with it. Sitting on the bank, opposite the gatehouse, and just outside the West Stenning boundary, was Julia.

Tom slowed to a trot, stopped and smiled. Julia scowled

at him. She had a radio balanced on her shoulder as if it were a ghetto blaster, and it was belting out raucous music, of the kind that, at home, came straight out of Karen's Walkman and into her ears. This radio was too small to be a real ghetto blaster but it was producing enough noise for Polly Ballard to appear at an upstairs window and slam it shut. Tom presumed that Julia was sitting in this particular place making that particular row expressly to annoy Polly. It was the kind of civil disobedience that appealed to him so he sat down too, a metre or so from Julia.

'My sister's bike turned up yet?'

Julia's scowl cobbled her forehead into pink corduroy.

'How should I know? Anyone'd think it was *worth* finding.'

'It's the only one she's got,' Tom said, looking poverty-stricken. 'It used to be my auntie's. Hannah wanted Karen's but she sold it to buy a Walkman.'

Julia was not interested in the problems of the lower orders. 'I expect Dina's out looking. She was all in a twist about it this morning.'

Tom looked hard at the radio.

'I'd have thought you'd have a Walkman,' he said.

'I have – at home,' Julia said, quickly. 'I've got my own music centre – at home.' She dumped the radio on to the grass where it continued to squawk and yodel. 'This old thing's Dina's.'

Tom knew perfectly well that it was Dina's. He remembered Dina, on her birthday, bringing it round to show Hannah, offering to lend it to Hannah. That had been during the poetry course. Dina had wanted a poet's autograph, the one who looked like a pickpocket. Tom had met him in Forstall Wood with a lady course member and the poet had not been very friendly. Mum said he had taken all the coat-hangers with him.

'It's quite new,' he said.

'It's rubbish,' Julia said. Tom stared at her until Julia began to fidget.

'Don't let me keep you,' said Julia.

'I'm meeting a friend,' Tom said. He unslung his binoculars and continued to examine Julia through them, the wrong way round. Julia dwindled, satisfyingly.

'Some people never know when they're not wanted,' Julia remarked.

Tom nodded. He was an expert at not being wanted.

'I've got better things to do than sit here talking to *you*,' Julia said, after a pause of some minutes in which neither of them said anything.

Tom shifted the binoculars and smiled politely. 'I expect so,' he said. Julia gave up. She rose to her feet and crossed the track to the wall where she had left her bicycle. At the same moment Polly Ballard came round the side of the gatehouse, wheeling *her* bicycle. It seemed to Tom that there was an epidemic of bicycles this summer. Polly and Julia glared at each other over the wall.

'This is a public road,' Julia declaimed, before Polly could say anything. 'You can't stop me sitting here.'

'I can stop you making that infernal racket,' Polly said, charging through the garden gate. She left her bicycle against the gatepost, and strode across the track, stooping over the bank to pick up the radio. 'I'm confiscating this,' Polly said.

'See if I care,' Julia said. She mounted and began pumping herself up the hill in the direction of the village. 'Anyone'd think it was mine.'

Polly stood watching her, jaws and fists clenched, the radio yowling under her arm. 'I'll kill her,' she said. 'So help me, I'll do her in.'

'That's Dina's radio,' Tom said, not wishing to be involved in a homicide.

'Oh hell, is it?' Polly laid it in the grass again, after switching it off. 'What's Julia doing with it?'

'I expect she pinched it,' Tom suggested. He was sure that Dina would not lend her precious radio even to Martin Carter's daughter. He recalled how relieved she had been when Hannah had declined the loan.

'You can give it back to her . . . can't you?' Polly mounted her bicycle and turned the handlebars towards the Challock Road. 'I mean, don't leave it there.'

'Aren't you going down to West Stenning today?' Tom asked.

'Not yet.' Polly was beginning to coast away. 'I'm going to see a friend in Molash.'

'What about George?'

'He's gone to Ashford – here!' Polly braked. 'What are you planning?'

'Nothing,' Tom said. He had not reached the planning stage, yet.

'You are *not* to go down to the manor.'

'I never do,' said Tom.

'No, sorry,' Polly said. She did not know the facts about the mousetraps.

When she was out of sight Tom turned his attention to the radio again. He remembered that it was also a cassette recorder and there was a tape in it. When he switched on nothing came out but a rasping hiss. Tom ran it back a way and tried again. He recognized the voice at once.

'. . . that's why I like going down to West Stenning. I don't really have any friends here and I've lived here since I was little.

'Julie's dad's serial was on again last night. I think it's brilliant but Julie said it couldn't be or they wouldn't put it on in the summer.

'While we were round by the church someone came and stole Hannah's bike. I haven't told her yet. She hasn't asked for it back yet. I don't know what I'll say when she does. I told the police. Sergeant Holdstock said someone was just mucking about probably but he wrote it all down.

'Mrs Ballard was horrible to me and Julie this morning. I don't want to go there again. Someone's coming. Bye.

'Saturday, 15 August. If Hannah asks for her bike back I'll have to say we're going out, or something. She won't ask for it this morning. They always go to Sainsbury's on Saturdays.'

Tom switched off. Saturday, 15 August? It was a diary! On tape. Tom would never have believed that Dina would have the wit to come up with an idea like that. It was brilliant. As he returned his finger to the switch he hesitated. He knew that it was wrong to *read* people's diaries because they were private, but this hardly counted as reading. It was more like a broadcast. He switched on again.

'I don't know what to do if it doesn't turn up. Hannah doesn't like me much anyway, she'll never let me go to West Stenning again, she thinks I'm stupid. Julie says I'm stupid, she says I'm retarded, I hate her, she was horrible to Mum this morning. I was sorry for her when she came because of her mum and dad being divorced but I don't care now. I hate her, she says horrible things, I hate her . . .'

Dina was crying. She must have forgotten that she was

recording herself because she cried for a long while before there was a click and the tape began hissing again. Tom switched off feeling really guilty now, because he had been eavesdropping, almost, and because he knew that what he had heard was true. No one was nice to Dina. Definitely he had better return the radio to her as soon as possible, preferably before she discovered that it was missing and went properly up the wall. He did not think he could cope with that.

Hannah was fetching the last of the shopping in from the boot when Tom cycled slowly past and stopped in the roadway, balancing on the pedals with his arm braced against the roof of the car.

'You seen Dina?' he said.

'Of course I haven't seen Dina. I've been to Ashford, haven't I? *Shopping*, haven't I?' They had come home to hear the bathwater running. Karen had just got up. 'She's probably looking for my bike.'

'Aren't you going to tell her you took it?'

'No. Why should I? She hasn't told me she's lost it.'

'Where've you hidden it?'

Hannah looked up sharply. 'None of your business. What do you want her for? You're not going to tell her I've got it, are you?'

'*Have* you got it?' Tom asked.

Hannah looked threatening. 'You keep out of this.'

'I'm not in it,' Tom said. He pushed himself away from the car and pedalled away towards the village. Hannah watched him go. What was he up to? He had been coming from Dina's end of the close when he stopped to talk. His rucksack hung across his back and the binoculars were slung about his neck as usual. The rucksack contained nothing but a rectangular object about the size of a dictionary; another bird book, no doubt.

'Tom!'

He stopped and looked around.

'Don't you dare tell Dina.'

'What?'

'About the bike.'

'Tell her what about the bike?'

'That I got it back.'

'Where is it?'

'Never you mind.'

'Well, I can't tell her then, can I?' Tom asked, reasonably.

'Why're you looking for her?'

'I've got something of hers,' Tom said. He indicated the rucksack and rode away. Hannah, satisfied, returned to the cereals and soap powders in the boot. Whatever Tom had in his rucksack, it wasn't a bicycle.

It was getting on for teatime before Tom found Dina. He saw her a long while before she saw him, approaching the crossroads, from the Ashford direction, poking in the ditch with a stick as policemen do when looking for corpses in rough country. A long sad shadow dragged itself behind her, almost too disheartened to keep up. Tom would not have been surprised to see it detach itself and lie down by the verge in despair.

'Lost something?' Tom asked, with a bright smile.

'It hasn't turned up, has it?' Dina looked almost hopeful. Tom would never have recognized in this tragic figure the pink and yellow vision that had coasted gaily down to West Stenning on Thursday.

'What?'

'Hannah's bike.'

'Oh, that. I thought you might be looking for this.' He took the rucksack from his shoulder and pulled out Dina's radio. Dina's eyes became perfectly round, like reflector studs. She grabbed the radio out of his hands.

'Whered' you get that?'

'Julia had it,' Tom said.

'What was she doing with it?'

'Listening to the radio, of course,' Tom said. 'It *is* a radio, isn't it?'

'It's a cassette recorder, too,' Dina said, and switched on, urgently. It hissed.

'Snakes?' Tom said.

Dina ignored him. She ran the tape back and tried again. There was a brief flash of Dina's own voice '– Ballard was horrible to me –' before she pressed the switch again.

'That was you!' Tom said, cleverly.

'It's private.' Dina cuddled the radio. 'I thought Julie must have been listening to it, it's the sort of thing she'd do. She keeps saying I read her diary. I *don't*. When did she have it?'

'This morning. Didn't you notice? That you didn't have it, I mean.'

'I haven't been home all day,' Dina said, forlornly. 'I've walked miles, looking for that bike. Is Hannah looking for *me*?'

'Oh, that.' Tom examined his fingernails, superbly casual. He had been practising for this moment. 'I found that, too.'

'Found it!' Dina clutched him and nearly dropped the radio. He had never noticed before how large Dina was; almost grown up; she engulfed him. 'Where is it?'

'Up on the downs,' Tom said, disengaging himself. 'In a holly bush. I expect someone took it for a laugh. It hasn't been vandalized or anything,' he added. A vandal would be hard put to know where to start on Hannah's old grid.

'You haven't told Hannah, have you?' Dina asked. 'She still thinks I've got it.'

'I expect she'd like to know where it is,' Tom said.

'Oh, *don't* tell her,' Dina begged. 'I'll get it back – you can show me where it is, can't you – oh!'

'Now what?' It was like talking to a grasshopper, the conversation leaping in unforeseen directions.

'I've got to get back. I'm going out – we all are. Martin Carter's taking us out to dinner in Canterbury. You couldn't get it for me, could you?'

'Not this evening,' Tom said, firmly.

'But Hannah's coming round for it.'

'But you'll be out,' Tom said.

'Oh . . . yeah. I don't want to go,' Dina said, her face falling again.

'I thought you liked Martin Carter.'

'I do. He's all right. But Julie's horrible, she's so rude to Mum. And me. I'm glad she's going on Monday,' Dina said.

'So's she, I bet,' Tom said, evilly.

'Can we go and get it tomorrow morning?'

'We're going to Folkestone all day if it stays fine,' Tom said. 'But you can find it. If you go up the path through Forstall Wood, past Lord Sherlock's bit, you'll come to a stile; you know? Where the path forks – one bit goes down to the manor. If you keep going along the edge of the field there's a sort of holly bush clump, on the right, behind the hedge. You can't miss it. The bike's in there.'

'Someone might have found it by then.'

'Shouldn't think so,' Tom said. 'It's the private part. No one goes there.'

'Someone did,' Dina said. 'I wonder who it was.'

'I wonder,' said Tom.

Chapter Eleven

Folkestone was not Hannah's favourite place, that would always be West Stenning, but she enjoyed a day out there, in summer; in winter it was like the end of the world. They did the same things every time; the beach in the morning, if the tide was out, before it became too crowded; then burgers or fish and chips for lunch and in the afternoon a round of pitch and putt on top of the cliffs, where there was always the feeling that if you hit the ball hard enough you could land it in the sea. Down below the Boulogne ferries went in and out. 'Not for much longer,' Tom regularly said. 'When they build the Channel Tunnel there won't be any ferries,' and Dad always said, 'Chance would be a fine thing.' Nothing changed.

Today she was particularly glad to be in Folkestone, away from the village, away from West Stenning, away from Dina, Julia and the bicycle. On the one hand Dina would have another day in which to fret – and after the way she sneaked off last night, serve her right – but on the other Hannah had an uneasy feeling that Sergeant Holdstock might be taking its disappearance seriously and begin making inquiries. She did not know if Dina had told him whose bicycle had gone missing; most likely not since he might well have suspected what had happened; it was his job to be suspicious.

As she walked round the pitch and putt course behind Dad – Mum and Tom were way out in front – she rehearsed the coming confrontation with Dina. If she went up to the wood as soon as they got home, around eight o'clock, she could ride down to the village, along the Challock Road, and ring Dina's stupid ding-dong-doorbell.

'Finished with my bike?' she would say, leaning negligently upon the handlebars, and what would poor Dina do then, poor thing? Burst into tears, no doubt, knowing Dina. She would be well and truly wound up by then anyway. With luck Dina should feel too ashamed to go anywhere near West Stenning for the rest of the week and after that she would be on her swanky holiday in Iesolo, wherever that was.

But she did wish Tom would stop giving her such funny looks. She was heartily glad that he was so far in front. Possibly he wasn't as daft as he seemed; possibly.

Rain was threatening by the time they reached home.

'What on earth do you want to go out now for?' Mum demanded, kicking a path to the sink through hillocks of Karen's dirty clothes that she had started to stuff into the washing machine and then abandoned.

'I just want a walk,' Hannah mumbled, also kicking the clothes, but only because they were there and because they were Karen's.

'You've been walking all *day*,' Mum said. She too had been walking all day; her feet hurt and the back of her neck was sunburned. 'Look, stop making a mess and put that lot back in the basket.'

''Snot my mess,' Hannah said, and made a great show of picking up the T-shirts and knickers with the washing tongs. As soon as Mum was in the front room finding out what Dad wanted for supper, she nipped out of the back door and up the garden to the rubbish heap. The sun was low, trapped in a narrowing crack between the clouds and the horizon; long shadows crept up the hillside from the houses behind her. Only the treetops in Sherlock's Wood caught the last orange glow, and by the time Hannah had reached the headland below the hedge the sun had set finally. The wood rustled suggestively and from Lord Sherlock's wheat came strange clicks and ticking. Down in the village late thrushes were still singing on the telephone wires. Up here the birds were silent.

The holly grove, always dark, looked black, menacing, in this light. Hannah remembered two things: first, that groves were once sacred to pagan gods and goddesses, where sacrifices were made and awful secret rites took place; second, that the holly was a holy tree, potent and ancient. No one ever cut down a holly tree. The grove murmured and closed in.

It was a long while before she could bring herself to squeeze under the thorn hedge. Even then she remained crouching to cross the cold soft squeaking leaves and reach out her hand to the place where she was sure she had left the bicycle; half expecting another hand to slide out of the darkness and grip it.

But there was nothing; no bicycle, no cold steel, no

chromium plate; only the sharp teeth of the holly leaves. Hannah had to stand up. Arms outstretched she circled in the gloom, hearing the wood beyond the grove crackle and sigh. There might be anything out there, anything in *here*, the place was shuffling, breathing; but there was no bicycle. In the darkness, in the woods, something screamed; maybe a vixen, maybe not. Hannah screamed too, and dived through the hedge, and ran.

Sunday, August 16th. If Julie's been listening to this I'll do *her. I don't think she has, though, she hasn't said anything, she just said she borrowed my radio and I said I know, ever so snarky, I said I think people who go into other people's rooms and take their things without asking are disgusting, I mean I was really rude and if she listened to the tape I'm sure she'd have said something then but she didn't. She was horrible when we went out to dinner last night but that was to her dad. She didn't talk to me at all. He was ever so embarrassed. He kept saying sorry. I'd be sorry if my daughter was like that. I wonder if her mum's like her.*

I've got the bike back. Tom Fisk told me about it, where it was. I wonder who put it there. It's the sort of thing Julie would do but she couldn't have because she was with me when it happened. I went up Lord Sherlock's wood this morning and it was just where Tom said, hidden in some holly bushes. It wasn't damaged or anything. I was going to take it back down through the wood and then I heard someone coming up the path. It was Karen Fisk and her boyfriend, that one from Chilham who comes over on a motor bike and wakes us all up at one in the morning. Dad says if he does it again he'll go down and drain his tank. I didn't know if Karen knew about the bike but I didn't want her to see me with it up in the woods so I went the other way. I had to lift it over the stile. It was dead heavy, it's quite old with floppy mudguards and an iron thing over the chain. It was just as well I did because Karen and her fellow started snogging or something. I don't know what but they stayed on the path. I couldn't see them, just giggles and snorting. She is thick. So's he or he wouldn't be her boyfriend.

Anyway, I went down through the sheep and then I saw the Ballards' Beetle coming down the track from the gatehouse. It's yellow, you can see it for miles. I didn't see who was driving it but I didn't want to run into Mrs Ballard, not after Thursday and I couldn't take the bike up to the woods again because of Karen, and then I ran into the other tutor, not Martin Carter, the one with the beard. And he said 'Hallo, what are you up to?' and I said I wanted to leave my friend's bike for her, I mean I couldn't think what to say; I didn't tell him which friend. He said 'All right. I'll put it in the stable for her,' and he took it away and I went all the way round through the sheep and out on to the track just past the cattle grid. I shut all the gates. You get murdered if you leave the gates open. They are Lord Sherlock's sheep. It would be awful if anything happened to them.

I wonder if there's a quick way down the hill to the village. It takes yonks on the footpath. I've got a blister. Bye.

Tom, on Monday's mousetrap detail, hid from an early morning course member in the old stable beneath the tutors' flat, and had his second unexpected encounter with Hannah's bicycle. It was lounging in a dark corner behind the Ford Transit and Martin Carter's Morris Traveller. He could not imagine why Drippy Dina should have left it there instead of taking it home with her, but no doubt it would be back in Hannah's possession quite soon and the incident would be closed. He set off up the track to collect *his* bicycle and, a hundred metres short of the gatepost, was forced on to the grass verge by the sudden appearance of a convoy of vehicles, juddering over the potholes in the direction of the manor. There were three vans, a minibus and a fleet of cars bringing up the rear. The driver of the first van braked sharply, causing all the others to do the same, and leaned out to call to Tom.

'Are we going the right way for West Stenning?'

'Down there.' Tom pointed. The driver looked unconvinced, but the convoy moved on again before Tom had a chance to ask if they were sure that West Stenning was where they wanted to go, and it was only after the last car had passed him that he registered the fact that the lettering on the minibus had read BBC TELEVISION. He was unimpressed, except by the thought, as he watched the vehicles bounce and crunch on the broken surface, that what West Stenning desperately needed was a really efficient road-building programme. The yard was nowhere near large enough to accommodate all those cars and vans, even if it were empty, and it was not. On Monday mornings the course members left, starting at around nine o'clock, in their own cars or in the Transit, driven by George who had yet to come down from the gatehouse. It would be too good to miss.

Tom left the track and moved across to a hillock in the pasture, among the sheep, which commanded a splendid view of the ballet of reverses and three-point turns that would be taking place shortly. His attention was absolute, so although he saw George go by in the yellow Volkswagen, he was too far from the gatehouse to see Dina turn off the Challock Road and on to the footpath through Forstall Wood, taking the long way round to recover Hannah's bicycle without running into Polly.

Hannah, squinting out of Mum's bedroom window, after

Mum had left for work, saw first Julia go past, on Dina's bicycle, and then Dina, on foot, also squinting, guiltily, in the direction of Hannah's front door.

Hannah was not lying in wait for Dina, she was looking out for Tom who had been in bed and conveniently asleep when she came down from the holly grove last night, and already up and out when she awoke this morning. She had persuaded herself that it was only panic that had prevented her from finding the bicycle, panic and bad light, but she felt very reluctant to visit the holly grove again just yet, because if the bicycle *wasn't* there it meant that someone else knew about the grove; someone who might be there before her.

Julia was almost certainly bound for West Stenning and it was an even bet that Dina was going the same way. Hannah left the window, bounded downstairs and out into the road, just in time to see Dina passing the Post Office, definitely heading for West Stenning. Keeping close to garden walls Hannah followed. Dina looked nervously over her shoulder once or twice, but she slowed down each time, giving Hannah a chance to shrink into the hedge.

Like this they passed the church, the pub and the pump. Dina turned right on to the Challock Road, Hannah followed grimly. Dina had a nerve. Going to the manor this way meant that she would have to pass the gatehouse and risk meeting Polly. Dina knew none of the dodges and short cuts, or so Hannah thought, but when she rounded the bend and came in sight of the gatehouse, Dina had vanished.

Hannah stopped. There were four ways that she could have gone; along the track, only she couldn't have passed out of sight already, along the Challock Road, down the path to the quarry or up the path through the woods. Then she saw a small figure sitting on a mound in the pasture, overlooking the manor; Tom. Hannah broke into a run.

Tom looked round as she came up behind him, grinned and pointed. Down below, in the yard of the manor, was the kind of traffic jam that normally happened only in Ashford on market days.

'What is it?' Hannah said, gazing at the vortex of vans and cars, with its tail that wound all the way back over the cattle grid where it was immobilized by the hill.

'Television,' Tom said happily. 'I thought they must have come the wrong way but they *asked* for West Stenning.'

Hannah recalled her conversation with George a week or two ago. 'That's right. They're filming today. Polly's furious.'

'Polly's always furious,' said Tom. 'Hey, I found your bike.'

'*You* found it?' Hannah almost hit him, remembering her terror last night. 'Why did you move it?'

'I never moved it,' Tom said. 'I left it where it was.'

'It's not there now.'

'Yes it is.'

'It *isn't.* I looked.'

'In the stable?'

'It's not in the stable,' Hannah shouted. 'In the holly grove, up Lord Sherlock's wood.'

'It was in the stable just now,' Tom said. He twirled a stalk of grass. 'I saw it.'

'My bike? In the stable?'

'That's right.'

'Are you sure?' Hannah was already on her way.

'Julia's down there,' Tom warned her.

'How d'you know?'

'She went down just now.'

'What about Dina?'

'Haven't seen Dina,' Tom said. At that moment he did see Dina, climbing over the stile at the top of the hill, but it seemed hardly worth the energy to complicate matters by pointing her out to Hannah. Things were coming nicely to the boil on their own. In any case, Hannah was getting up speed, aiming straight for the cattle grid although she would never be able to get into the yard that way. Tom could see, as she could not, one of the television vans wedged firmly between the gateposts.

She disappeared briefly from sight round the corner, at about the same time that Dina also vanished behind the house. Tom leaned back on his elbows and debated odds on which of them would reach the bicycle first. His money was on Dina for Hannah suddenly reappeared, running round the line of the hedge that separated the manor garden from the pasture. The gate, that was supposed to be kept firmly shut, was standing open, as Julia had left it, five minutes earlier, when she wheeled Dina's bicycle through it having found the gateway blocked. Hannah would have trouble following, though. As soon as Julia had gone through, the sheep, hanging about as usual waiting for something to happen, had finally been rewarded. First one, then another, and at last the whole flock, began crowding through the gap, round the end of the barn and into the yard. Tom stared, entranced. It was better than *The Great Escape*. There were about forty people in the yard, including Julia, George, Mum, Gavin Russell, a dozen vehicles and fifty sheep. He had counted them through the gate.

The only person he would have expected to see, and did not, was Dina; but after a few minutes he noticed her on the footpath, pushing Hannah's bicycle over Fylde Brook Bridge.

All Hannah could think was, 'Thank goodness Polly isn't here.' George, spinning around in the middle of the mêlée, was clearly enjoying himself in a mad sort of way. Chaos got his adrenalin going; she had noticed that before. Hannah dared not think what Polly might have done, might do yet, if she should turn up. As she squeezed through the sheep and behind the television vans, keeping well out of Mum's view, she realized for the first time how strange it was that Polly had *not* come out, for Monday was one of her busiest times, but once she reached the stable she forgot all about Polly. Martin Carter's Morris Traveller and the Transit were out in the yard, and her bicycle was not there either. The stable was empty, as empty as the holly grove had been. The only bicycle of any description, anywhere, was Dina's, and Julia had that out in the yard.

The door at the top of the stairs opened and Martin Carter came down, carrying a suitcase. He looked even more defeated than usual.

'Good morning,' he said, when he saw Hannah, for he always remembered his manners. 'Are you looking for something?'

'My bike,' Hannah said.

'If it weren't for Julia,' said Martin Carter, 'I'd borrow your bike and ride to Ashford station. I've got to be in London by eleven-thirty.'

'What about your car?' Hannah said. She looked where he was looking, at the solid jam of vehicles. 'You're stuck.'

'So I am,' he said, heavily.

'Where is it?'

'God knows; swept away, I should think.' He went back up a few steps. 'Over there, by the barn. I think I recognize its roof.'

'There's another way out,' Hannah said. 'Through the gate the sheep came in by. You'll have to drive across the field but you can join the track further up.'

'Can you show me?'

'Can I come with you?'

'You'll have to. I don't know the way.'

Mum had gone indoors again to answer the telephone. Hannah dived among the sheep and round the television vans, keeping one eye on the kitchen door and hoping that Martin Carter was following. He was, and somewhere along the line he had collected Julia.

'I'm not *ready*,' Julia was yelling. 'I came down by *bike*! Anyone'd think –'

'Oh, belt up!' her father roared, startling the sheep. 'Do as you're told for once and stop arguing.' It wasn't a patch on Major Nevard but it was certainly an improvement on Martin Carter. It was almost as good as Mum. They piled into the Morris Traveller. 'We'll stop off at the Swains' and collect your stuff, Julia. JULIA! Stop grizzling.'

The car began to edge coyly towards the gateway.

'If you hadn't left that damn gate open this wouldn't have happened,' Martin Carter said. 'And don't imagine that you can ever try anything like this again.'

'I wanted to see you,' Julia wailed.

'You saw me last week.'

'Nobody cares about me. You sent me away –'

'I did not!'

'You sent me to boarding school.'

'I did not send you to boarding school. I can't afford to

send you to boarding school. *I* never went to boarding school, you begged to go.'

'I hate it.'

'Well leave then. Your mother hates it, too. She misses you.'

'No she doesn't. She's got Michael Atkins.'

'No she hasn't. What *is* all this about Michael Atkins?'

'She's going to marry him.'

'She is not going to marry him. She hardly knows him.'

'But he came to our house –'

'They work together, that's all. Julia, you must stop fantasizing –'

They swerved to avoid a sheep.

'Look, Julia,' he said, more gently, now that they were clear of the gate, 'it's no good making yourself miserable just to make us miserable. You always suffer most. If you want to make us suffer you'll have to think of a better way.'

'Didn't you suffer this weekend?'

'Not as much as Mrs Swain did,' said Martin Carter. He steered the car over the bumpy pasture one-handed, and put his arm round Julia. Extremely dangerous, Hannah thought, but they had forgotten about her, sitting in the back seat, until she tapped him on the shoulder and said, 'Turn right, here.'

He guided the car back on to the track, just where the tail-back ended with George's yellow Volkswagen. On the horizon a figure strolled leisurely towards the woods, accompanied by an alien quadruped that seemed to have one horn growing out of its shoulders.

'Did I see that or did I see that?' Martin Carter said, risking a sideways look at the ambling group. 'Oh, it's that strange child who wants to build a bypass.'

'It's my brother,' Hannah said. 'He's bird-watching.' She had identified the group as Tom and a lone sheep that had missed the fun. On its back rode Ogmore. He was washing, head down, with one leg raised sedately in the air. A bypass? She decided that they didn't come any stranger than Martin Carter.

On the kitchen table was a note, left by Mum, which Hannah had failed to find earlier. *Hannah: please get cut loaf, ½ lb luncheon meat, 5 lb spuds from Suzie. Money on window sill.*

She found a fiver tucked under the coffee jar, picked out a plastic carrier from the collection under the sink and set out for the shop. The Carters had gone. There had been no one at home when they stopped to collect Julia's holdall. Julia said Mrs Swain had gone to work. Hannah thought she was more likely hiding from Julia, as Dina was hiding from Hannah, but as she neared the shop she saw something that she had long ago given up expecting to see; Dina, riding Hannah's bicycle, coming down from West Stenning.

'You finished with it, then?' Hannah said.

'Yes. Thanks.' They stared at each other, each wondering how much the other one knew.

'Where's yours?'

'Julie took it down the manor this morning,' Dina said. 'Do you know if she's come back?'

'They've gone,' Hannah said. 'They went just now. She left your bike in the yard. I'll fetch it back later, if you like.'

'Thanks,' Dina said. 'Shall I come too?'

'Better not.'

'No . . . well . . .'

'You know . . . Polly . . .'

'Yeah.'

'See you, then.'

'See you.'

Hannah went into the shop. No more Dina. No more Dina hanging about wearing loopy clothes, hoping for autographs, getting in the way. And if she could promise Polly that there would be no more Dina, perhaps Polly would relent and allow her to go back to West Stenning. The shop went suddenly dark. Hannah, about to leave, opened the door and saw the Ashford bus stopping outside. Polly was getting off it; Polly, beaming. When she saw Hannah coming out of the shop she swung round and laughed.

'Hannah!'

Hannah advanced cautiously, crabwise.

'Where've you been?'

'Only to the doctor's.'

'The doctor's?'

'I'm all right. Really I'm all right. Oh, Hannah, I'm going to have a baby.' Polly flung her arms round Hannah and hugged her. Hannah, astonished, hugged her back. She had never done that to a grown-up before, except Mum and Dad and Gran. It felt strange, even though Polly was so small.

'When?'

'Middle of March. Isn't it wonderful?'

Hannah could think only of West Stenning, the course members, the television people, the sheep. George. Wonderful? She said, 'A baby?'

'Yes.'

'A baby – and George?'

'Don't be such a downer. We've been trying for years.'

Definitely Polly had better not go back to West Stenning just yet. 'Come home,' Hannah said. 'I'll make you a cup of tea to celebrate.'

'Oh yes, please.' Polly was almost dancing along beside her. 'No more booze for a bit, not even to celebrate. George can give it up too – keep me company.'

'Will you stay on . . . at West Stenning?'

'For a while. Why not?'

'Won't it be too much?'

'We'll have to see. Stop being so practical, Hannah. I'm so pleased and silly about it I can't think straight.'

'I can help . . . more,' Hannah offered.

'You *do* help. I'm sorry I was such a crab last week, but I've felt so rotten and I couldn't be absolutely certain – why I felt rotten, I mean. Keep coming – of course you must. Why don't you let Dina give a hand too?'

'Dina?'

'If we *asked* her along she might not hang about so much looking wistful,' Polly said. 'She seems to like the place as much as you do.'

You can say that again, Hannah thought, crossly. All that trouble to keep Dina away and here she was, being asked to invite her. Still, it might mean less effort in the long run, once Dina had recovered from Julia Carter. Later she would walk back to West Stenning with Polly and collect Dina's bicycle. Then she could take it round to Number Ten and perhaps invite Dina to come and watch episode four of *Decisions* tonight. It would be a peace offering and, in any case, more fun than watching it with Karen and Tom. Karen was a zombie and Tom – Tom wasn't much better. He lived in a world of his own. Look at him all this last weekend, drifting about with his binoculars. He hadn't a clue what had been going on.

Mrs Nevard was learning how the other half lived. Daily she toiled at her factory bench, inspecting aircraft engines, dressed in oily overalls and with her hair done up in a turban. After the hooter went she clocked out with all the other weary women and fought her way on to a tube train. One evening Major Nevard was standing on the platform being passionate with his army lady when a train pulled in and the doors opened and there was Mrs Nevard, asleep in a corner seat looking old and plain in her turban and overalls and nasty green cloth coat. Major Nevard gasped, stiffened, slapped the Old Wound and leaped on to the train as the doors were closing, leaving his army lady distraught upon the platform. He had made another decision.

Karen, watching, thought, 'Oh yeah?' and put a fresh cassette in her Walkman.

Dina thought: 'Julie was right, it is rubbish. If Mrs Ballard has a baby she might let me help look after it. I wish Mum would have another baby.'

Hannah thought: 'Julia's dad should have yelled at her *years* ago. She liked it. Only children are always spoiled . . . not Dina though. I thought she was but she isn't. Not like Julia. I was rotten to her. She's not that bad . . .'

Tom thought: 'If you can send the hedgehogs through a concrete pipe, why not the whole road? If you can have a Channel Tunnel, why not a Stour Valley Tunnel? Why not put *everything* underground and link Dover to Dartford?' A maze of burrows formed before his eyes, quite like a bird's intestines but much more convoluted. He saw headlines in the *Kent Messenger*: REPRIEVE FOR LOCAL BEAUTY SPOT, and all due to Tom Fisk: T. J. Fisk, ARIBA.

'I've been living in a dream world. I'm awake now, I can see again. I love only you, darling,' said Major Nevard.

Some other books you might enjoy

JUNIPER

Gene Kemp

Since her dad left, Juniper and her mum have had nothing but problems and now things are just getting worse – there are even threats to put Juniper into care. Then she notices two suspicious men who seem to be following her. Who are they? Why are they interested in her? As Christmas draws nearer, Juniper knows something is going to happen . . .

THE SEA IS SINGING

Rosalind Kerven

Tess lives right in the north of Scotland, in the Shetland Islands, and when she starts hearing the weird and eerie singing from the sea it is her neighbour, old Jacobina Tait, who helps her understand it. With her strange talk of whales and 'patterns' Jacobina makes Tess realize that she cannot – and must not – ignore what the singing is telling her. But how can Tess decipher the message?

RACSO AND THE RATS OF NIMH

Jane Leslie Conly

When fieldmouse Timothy Frisby rescues young Racso, the city rat, from drowning, it's the beginning of a friendship. It's also the beginning of Racso's education – and an adventure. For the two are caught up in the brave and resourceful struggle of the Rats of NIMH to save Thorn Valley, their home, from destruction.

A TASTE OF BLACKBERRIES

Doris Buchanan Smith

The moving story about a young boy who has to come to terms with the tragic death of his best friend and the guilty feeling that he could somehow have saved him.